The Failed

W.J. Small

Copyright © W.J. Small 2022.

The right of W.J. Small to be identified as the author of this work has been asserted by her in accordance with the Copyright, Designs and Patents Act, 1988.

First published in 2022 by Sharpe Books.

To my parents,
for their love, encouragement, and support,
their laughter and their guidance.

I will clamber through the clouds and exist.
 - John Keats

THE FAILED APPRENTICE

Chapter 1

Life changed for Will Patten the night his master disappeared into the Thames.

George Topside was a blacksmith in London, a widower with whom Will had apprenticed for the last four years. A man skirting the end of middle age, Topside was a fine craftsman but had a lucrative side business as well. That dark night, his side business caught up with him.

Will was following Topside through the London streets, back to the blacksmith shop, but keeping a respectable distance to allow for spying. Topside had been acting cagey lately; Will was sure something was amiss and, if it affected his future, wanted to know what was causing Topside's change in behavior. The full moon slid behind a cloud, and in that moment of half-darkness, two men emerged from the shadows and sidled up to Topside. Will stopped, then inched closer to try and hear the conversation.

There was no conversation, though. Instead, the taller man grabbed Topside by the arm; Topside jumped and tried to wrench free. A scuffle ensued with Topside on the losing end. Will heard Topside cry for help, but that was quickly extinguished when the shorter man produced a cudgel and struck Topside over the head. The thump bounced off nearby buildings, and Will, stunned, retreated deeper into the shadows. Topside crumpled at the man's feet, a lifeless heap. The men picked up Topside by his limp arms and flung his inert body into the Thames, splashing solidly into the river, which already smelled of refuse, the contents of chamber pots, and dead animals.

Shaking, Will watched as the two men peered over the small embankment, making sure Topside was dead and, hopefully, floating away. Satisfied, they nodded and slapped each other on the back. Then they turned and headed down the street, disappearing into the nearest pub.

Will did not particularly like George Topside. Although related to the Pattens by marriage, Topside had been stingy with sharing his knowledge and his food with Will. Like all apprentices, Will lodged in his master's home. But his small bedroom, a dark chamber in a low-ceilinged garret, was infested with a family of mice. Will's room was cold in the winter and hot in the summer, and his one window provided little ventilation. Still, it was a job, and Will knew once his apprenticeship was over, he could make a good living as a blacksmith in Henry VIII's England.

Will turned and scurried back to Topside's home, trying to push his fear aside. Instead, he tried to sort through his next steps now that Topside was, presumably, dead. He hoped he had learned enough to run Topside's forge and could step in once it was clear Topside was gone for good. However, as he rounded the corner, he noticed a thin curl of smoke wafting skyward, punctuated by several errant sparks. Somewhere down the road there was a fire, and Will had a sinking feeling he knew where. Moments later, he heard cries of "Fire! Fire!" and the crackling of old timber. As Will approached, his fears were confirmed; it was Topside's home, rapidly engulfed in flames.

Will raced to the house. Fire lit the home's interior, already charring the first floor windows and illuminating the front room. Will's few possessions were in the attic, from where a serpentine tongue of flame licked outwards. He lunged toward the door but was held back by a pair of strong hands. "What do you think you're doing? The house is on fire," the man holding him exclaimed.

"But my things," Will said. "Everything I own is inside!" Will looked toward the garret; an orange flame flickered out the window. Moments later, the roof collapsed.

"Not anymore," the man replied, releasing his grasp on Will.

Neighbors arrived, and buckets of water were thrown on the flames but to no avail. Within minutes, the house was reduced to a few skeletal timbers and a pile of ash. The water was successful only in putting out the few embers still burning and keeping the

THE FAILED APPRENTICE

fire from spreading to nearby homes. For the neighbors, this was a success. But for Will, it was a total loss.

Topside's forge was next to the house, and Will hoped it survived the blaze. But the forge had been burned, and the surviving tools smashed and bent, rendering them useless. What was left would be costly to fix, repairs that Will had no funds to pay for. He kicked around the dirt floor, but all that remained were ashes surrounding useless metal shards.

As Will continued to search the room, he felt a presence moving behind him. He turned to see Topside's neighbor, Edward Kelley, approach. Will had always liked Kelley, who occasionally shared bread and cheese with the struggling apprentice. "Will," Kelley said, concern resonating in his voice. "I'm relieved to see you. I was afraid you'd been burned alive."

"I wasn't here when the fire started," Will replied, his voice shaky. "What happened?"

Kelley looked around nervously. Inching closer to Will, he lowered his voice. "Two men came by earlier, looking for Topside. They created a ruckus. When they couldn't find him, they started destroying the forge. Then they moved on to the house. I tried to get a good look at them, but they kept to the shadows."

Will nodded. Topside had clearly fallen on the wrong side of some dangerous men.

"I think it may have something to do with his business in Southwark," Kelley continued. "They didn't look like the gentlemen who normally visit the forge."

"I'm sure you're right," Will said. Topside's salacious dealings across the Thames were the worst kept secret amongst his neighbors. "Thank you for letting me know what happened."

Kelley looked at Will with pity in his eyes. "Do you need anything, Will? An extra set of clothes? A coin or two?"

Although Will needed both, he shook his head. "Thank you for the offer, but I'll be fine."

"And Topside?" Kelley continued. "Where is the lout?"

Will did not have the heart, nor the stomach, to tell Kelley what happened to his master. Instead, he shook his head. "I haven't seen him," he muttered.

"Well, he'll be in for a sad surprise," Kelley said as he turned to walk back to his home.

Will assessed his surroundings. Both house and forge were destroyed. So that was that – more than four years of his life was floating down the Thames and in the wet ash of a burned house. Will had nowhere to go but home.

It was a long way back to Fenn Road, the street of his childhood home. Fenn was a short street, barely more than an alley, with uneven stones separated by caked dirt. Fenn's claim to fame was in its name, though. The road was named after a 14th-century serf who ran away from his master to seek his fortune in London. He ultimately found success as a huckster, eventually becoming prosperous enough to buy a small shop and home on the very street where Will lived. Yet that morning, the ambitious serf was the last thing on Will's mind as he walked the cold and dangerous streets, slipping into shadows and alleys when he sensed danger. The sun was rising as he turned onto Fenn, casting long shadows on the narrow roadway.

The Pattens' house was small and timber-framed, stylish when built but had since seen wear. The door hung loosely on its hinges, and the house had begun shifting precipitously to the right. As a result, the floors were at an angle and made balancing tricky, especially after returning home from the tavern. Will pulled the thin oak door open, noticing the cracks in the wood which let in the summer air. Although it was early, his mother was up with her youngest child, a baby who was sucking on a rag soaked in mead.

"Will," Elizabeth Patten said, startling slightly as Will walked into the dark front room of the house. "What are you doing here? Shouldn't you be at the forge?"

Will looked around the room. The Pattens were not wealthy; Will's father, Peter, was a draper who had a consistent business selling cloth. Although he had a steady stream of customers, most were financially strapped, which led to the Pattens constantly

THE FAILED APPRENTICE

teetering above the poverty line and the business barely solvent. Yet if Peter and Elizabeth Patten had stuck to just one or two children, they might have been considered well off. But Kate, now gumming a rag on her mother's lap, was the Pattens' seventh child, taxing the family's finances even more.

"Topside was killed," Will said, pulling up a wooden chair, one leg significantly shorter than the others. "His home was burned. The forge, too. Destroyed."

"What happened?" Elizabeth asked, clutching Kate tighter.

"He got on the wrong side of some ruffians," Will said. "He ended up in the Thames."

"Dear God." Elizabeth shook her head. "I knew that man's ways would catch up to him. My cousin should have left well enough alone and never married him."

Although a successful blacksmith, George Topside's true claim to fame was his lucrative business in Southwark. Owner of the Sharpened Axe, a mid-sized brothel located down an alley in an area populated with other brothels, cock fighting, and gambling, Topside had been able to turn his small investment into a sizable profit. Although he had to pay taxes on the brothel - most notably to the Bishop of Winchester, in whose jurisdiction Southwark lay - he also managed to pocket a tidy sum. But the prostitution business was not without its dangers. The Axe attracted men who leaned toward brutality, and it was not unusual for fights to break out in the brothel, knives being drawn, blood being spilled.

Topside had occasionally dispatched Will to the Axe to collect money and check on Ellyn, the woman who oversaw the brothel's day-to-day operations. Having aged out of prostitution herself, Ellyn was a shrewd businesswoman who tolerated little from both the women in her employ and the men who frequented them. Tall, wide, and tougher than most of her clientele, Ellyn was not above chasing a cheating client out of her brothel with a knife, cudgel, or any other weapon within her reach.

"Will, what are you doing here?" Peter Patten said, entering the room, daybreak filtering in through the small windows, lighting his lined face.

"Topside is dead," Elizabeth interjected. "His house burned. The forge destroyed."

Peter sighed and looked questioning at Will.

"I had nowhere else to go," Will said.

"This is most unfortunate," Peter replied. "We just got rid of Osman. Now you are back."

Osman was Will's younger brother who, after proselytizing the family with his religious zeal for years, had left to become a monk. Will never understood his brother's unwavering and absolute faith, but that did not matter. The Pattens were just glad to have him out of the house.

Peter shifted his weight from one foot to the other and looked pointedly at Will. Tall and thin, he was not an old man, but caring for a large family on a small income had taxed him. His face was prematurely etched in wrinkles, and he was perpetually tired and awoke every morning looking defeated before the day had even begun.

"I'll find something else," Will said. "I don't expect you to support me."

"Will, you can take Osman's pallet," Elizabeth said. "Stay here until you work this out."

Peter looked at Will. "You may stay here," he said. "But you need to bring in some money. I can't afford to clothe another body and feed another mouth."

Will nodded. Peter turned and left the room, shaking his head.

Will spent his first day at home sleeping on Osman's pallet, cramped in a room barely larger than a closet that Osman had shared with younger brother John. Yet Will slept soundly, exhausted from the previous night's activities. Peter finally roused him the next morning. "Get up," he said, toeing the bed.

Will rolled off the pallet and scratched his head. His hair felt greasy, and his clothes smelled of smoke and ash. "I'm up," he said, yawning.

"You need to go to the Blacksmith Guild this morning. They should be able to find you a placement. You are already more than halfway through your training."

THE FAILED APPRENTICE

Will looked around the room, dawn edging through jagged cracks in the timber. He stretched his arms over his head, his stomach grumbling. "Will, get going," Peter said. "This is not an inn. It is not my job to keep a roof over your head."

With that, a baby's cry seeped through the thin wall separating Will from his family. Peter gave Will one last meaningful look and, with shoulders stooped, walked from the room.

The Blacksmith Guild was south of Fenn Road, off St. Peter's Hill near the Thames, a fifteen-minute walk. Will grabbed a heel of bread from the larder and picked off the mold growing on one of its corners. Heading toward the guild, he thought of his parents - once respected, even bordering on well-to-do. Now, burdened with too many mouths to feed and a faltering business, they were well on their way to becoming one of London's many poverty-stricken families, struggling just to survive. When Will was young, Peter was an engaged father, spending his free time playing with him or teaching him to read from the hornbook. Now, his father barely interacted with his youngest children, regarding them with an undercurrent of resentment. Will resolved to not make the same mistakes.

Chapter 2

The Blacksmith Guild was an old building, a wattle and daub structure that had settled, the limewash fading to a dirty mustardy yellow. Will entered the low-ceilinged front room, a large desk in its center, where a young clerk sat, his face lit by a flickering candle.

"May I be of assistance?" The clerk asked, eyeing Will up and down. "Perhaps you are lost?"

Will was aware he looked and smelled like an aging street urchin. Standing tall, he replied, "I am Will Patten, apprentice to George Topside."

The clerk's eyes widened. "Topside's body was pulled from the Thames yesterday. He was quite dead."

Will nodded. Topside's body had been recovered. Maybe that would work to Will's advantage. A dead master was better than a missing one. "I know, and I'm sorry for the loss, but I am now out of a job and need a new master," Will said.

The clerk coughed and opened a voluminous tome. Rifling through the pages, he finally found what he was looking for, his finger tracing down a long list of names. "Ah, there you are, William Patten, son of Peter, apprentice to George Topside."

"Yes, that's me."

Again, the clerk coughed. "Excuse me for a moment," he replied, closing the book, standing, and walking toward a dark room deeper into the guildhall.

While Will waited, he looked around the room. The guildhall was old - for at least a hundred years, blacksmiths had met, paid their dues, and fraternized there, bonding over shared work. The walls were lined in soot, the windows glassed but grimy. A fire burned in a small stone fireplace, its flames barely warming the room.

THE FAILED APPRENTICE

Moments later, the clerk returned, followed by an older man with an air of authority about him. He sized Will up before speaking. "William Patten?"

"Yes."

"I am Michael Graybridge, Chief Warden of the Blacksmith Guild. Unfortunately, there seems to be a problem with your apprenticeship."

"Well, my master is dead," Will said. "I would say that's a problem."

Graybridge cleared his throat. "It seems George Topside hadn't paid his guild dues in," the warden looked down at the parchment clenched in his hand, "two years. He was given multiple warnings. A note in the margin says he just didn't care."

Will had heard Topside rail against the guild on more than one occasion. Topside said he would not pay his dues, would not attend religious services, would not meet with his peers in the guildhall. At the time, Will believed this to be mere bluster. Clearly, it was not. "Where does that leave me?" Will asked.

"I'm afraid it leaves you out in the cold," Graybridge said. "Topside was expelled from the guild a month ago. You didn't know?"

Will looked down at his shoes, scuffed and covered in dust. "Topside shared very little with me," Will said. "I had no idea."

The warden sighed. "He was hoping for free labor before it became obvious that he was out of the guild. I can see if any of my smiths will take you on, but we are not beholden to you since Topside was no longer a member."

"I understand. I do have almost five years of training," Will said, almost as an afterthought.

"Duly noted. Stop by tomorrow. I'll see what I can do," Graybridge said as he turned and walked back to the room from where he had come.

Will left the guildhall and turned east toward Queenhithe. Heavy clouds were forming over the city, bulbous and dark, the air thick with an impending storm. Although Will should have headed home, he continued along the Thames, watching the wherries transporting passengers along the river. The river was teeming with boats, both large and small. There were so many you could almost step your way from one to another to cross the Thames.

Will remembered when he began his work with Topside. At fourteen, he was propelled into the world of blacksmithing after his older brother Peter followed in his father's footsteps by apprenticing as a draper. Will had only a passing knowledge of Topside, the older man his aunt had married, the aunt who had died the following year of sweating sickness. But Topside needed an apprentice, and the Pattens wanted to get their second son out of the house and established in a trade.

Foolishly, Will expected to be working the forge, creating intricate weapons and armor, immediately. Instead, he was tasked with keeping the forge, and Topside's house, clean. The second year Topside allowed Will to forge nails and basic cutlery. When Will asked to help with more specialized work, Topside smacked him on the head with a heavy glove. "You be getting ahead of yourself, you little cur," Topside said, sneering at Will.

Although Will had worked for Topside for close to five years, he had gained little knowledge and experience. Will knew how to keep the forge working, the fires appropriately hot, the tools clean. But aside from teaching Will to craft nails, trinkets, and a few household items, Topside withheld his knowledge. Even if the guild found Will a placement, he knew he was well behind where he should be in the world of the blacksmith.

Then there was Topside's other business, the Sharpened Axe. Will knew a bit more about that. Topside was quick to dispatch Will to Southwark whenever he felt something was amiss at the brothel or simply to collect money from Ellyn. Will had become proficient at minor repairs to the structure - repairing a wall with a nail he had crafted at the forge, fixing a step that a client had fallen through, installing latches on the doors and windows. He would give the guild one more day. He would return in the morning, and if they had not found him a placement, he would head to the Axe and see what Ellyn could do for him.

THE FAILED APPRENTICE

Will returned home just as dusk was settling over London. Elizabeth had prepared a meager supper, and she, Peter, and their children were gathered around the rough trestle table in the front room. Will took his seat and ran his hand over the knife marks and darkened stains which covered the table's surface.

As Elizabeth served a thin pottage into small, wooden bowls, Peter addressed Will. "How was the meeting with Blacksmith Guild? Did they find you a placement?"

Will watched as his mother's eyes looked at Will, then moved quickly to Peter, and then back to the bowl of food. Will cleared his throat. "It seems as though Topside hadn't paid his dues in a couple years. He was expelled from the guild right before his death."

Peter brought his hands down onto the table so forcefully that the bowls rattled, and the baby began to scream. "And this leaves you where?" Peter barked. "Out in the cold?"

"I need to return tomorrow," Will said. "They're trying to find me a placement with another smith."

Peter turned to Elizabeth. "Your worthless cousin! If she hadn't married that arse Topside, Will wouldn't be in this position."

Elizabeth raised herself up and glared at Peter. "You leave Anne out of it! She loved George." Elizabeth hesitated. "He was charming once - rich too. We thought he was a good catch at the time."

"And look how that turned out," Peter said, scowling at Elizabeth, then returning his glare to Will. "You best get over there early and remind them of the time you've already put in," he said. "That should count for something."

"I already did," Will said, trying to shut out Kate's screams and his father's steady stare.

Although hungry after wandering the streets for most of the day, Will looked at the thin stew in front of him and had no appetite. A few beans floated on the top, and stringy cabbage and limp oats swirled as Will stirred the broth. He looked around the table. Kate was crying, Peter was scowling, and Elizabeth was holding back tears. His brothers, oblivious to the drama unfolding, were pinching each other under the table. Will stood up and left the room.

The following day Will woke before the sun was up. He washed his face and dried it with his soiled shirt, which still smelled of smoke from Topside's fire. Then, tiptoeing over the sleeping John, he crept out of the tiny room and toward the door. He would leave for the guild before his family awoke. The thought of his father looking at him with sad, disappointed eyes was more than Will could bear at that early hour.

Fog swirled around the London streets as Will walked toward the Thames. The morning was cool, and moisture clung to Will's clothing, making his thin shirt and breeches uncomfortably damp. When he arrived at the guild, the door was locked with a rusty padlock. Will wondered if the lock was created at Topside's forge, but, given Topside's relationship with the guild, decided it probably wasn't.

After waiting close to an hour, a figure emerged from the fog, the noise of keys clanging together heralding his arrival. It was Michael Graybridge.

"Master Graybridge," Will said, stepping out from the doorway. "I've come to see about a placement."

"Ah, Will," Graybridge said, turning a heavy iron key in the padlock's keyhole. "Topside's apprentice. You are up early. Come in."

Will followed Graybridge into the darkened room, which smelled of fire and ash, even though embers in the hearth had long been extinguished. The sun was rising and burning off the fog, but the room remained dark except for a thin shaft of light filtering from the windows. "Sit," Graybridge said, motioning to a sturdy chair in front of the clerk's desk.

Will sat and looked at Graybridge, who sighed deeply as he sat behind the desk. "I've spoken with a few peers, men who are sympathetic to your situation," he began.

Will leaned forward, hopeful.

THE FAILED APPRENTICE

"Yet," Graybridge said, tenting his hands on the top of the desk, "Topside's reputation is a strike against you. No one wants to be associated with a man who ended up floating in the Thames."

"I had nothing to do with that," Will said. Then remembering his father's words, added, "My training with Topside must count for something."

"I understand," Graybridge continued. "But Topside's attitude toward the guild, his reputation of being a poor master, and his affiliation with the Axe are more than any of my smiths can look past."

Will looked down at his hands. They were worn and calloused, although not as calloused as they should have been after more than four years as a blacksmith's apprentice. "I think I'd make the same decision if I were in their shoes," he admitted.

Graybridge stood, prompting Will to do the same. "I wish you the best, Will," he said. "I'm sorry you are in such a situation."

Will nodded. "Thank you for trying," he said as he turned to leave.

Will wandered the streets for an hour, trying to devise a new plan. Ellyn and the Axe had been lurking in the back of his mind. He had not been to the brothel in several weeks; undoubtedly, something needed fixing. He would head over there after dinner.

The noon meal at the Pattens was as sparse as supper the night before. Elizabeth served the same tepid cabbage stew with an onion and beef bone added since the previous night. Accompanying the pottage was bread, clearly not fresh; it took effort for Will to tear a piece from the loaf. Elizabeth bounced Kate on her lap, dipping a morsel of bread in the broth and feeding it to the child. Will's brothers sat at the table, taking turns hitting each other on the arm. "You flinched!" John said triumphantly after landing a strong blow on his brother, Mark's, forearm. Mark responded by hitting John in the head.

"I returned to the Blacksmith Guild this morning," Will began. Peter looked at him hopefully. "They have nothing for me. Topside is a black mark they can't look past."

"I thought that might be the case," Peter said, ignoring his younger sons who continued to smack each other. "I went to my guild this morning, hoping to find you a new apprenticeship if the blacksmiths fell through. But you, you are too old to begin anew. No one wants an apprentice approaching his twentieth year. And your training is in smithing." Peter was a member of the Worshipful Company of Drapers and, unlike Topside, was well-regarded and participated in regular meetings. Although barely able to feed his family, Peter was current with his guild dues.

Will nodded. He had been expecting as much.

Peter sighed. "I don't know what to tell you, Will. Perhaps you could work as a servant? You could talk to Amy. See if the master of the house needs help."

Amy was Will's younger sister who had recently begun domestic work at a wealthy merchant's home on London Bridge. Although probably the most intelligent of the Patten children, Amy was messy, careless, and impulsive. But she was kind, and her sense of humor was quick and biting.

"Will?" Peter continued. "What about it? Asking Amy?"

Will grunted. He was not cut out to be a servant. He had tasted some freedom at Topside's; he was not about to be placed in another, stronger yoke. "Perhaps," he said. "I may have another lead."

"If something does not come up by week's end," Peter said. "You best be asking Amy."

Will ignored his father and watched his two small brothers. They had left the table and now sat on the packed dirt floor. A bruise was already forming on Mark's forearm. Will watched as they rolled a ball of discarded fabric around the floor; the material, once colorful, was faded, dirty, and torn. The ball rolled precipitously close to the fire, whose embers glowed dully but cast no heat. "Get that ball away from the ashes," Peter yelled, standing up from the table and heading to the door. He turned and faced Will. "I am going back to work, but I want news tonight, Will. I want a plan for your future."

THE FAILED APPRENTICE

Chapter 3

Will left soon after his father. The walk to the Axe was not difficult, and Will followed the narrow, circuitous streets toward London Bridge, which would take him to Southwark.

London Bridge was busy that afternoon. Those traveling to and from Southwark were noisy as they crowded together on the roadway. Large homes, some six stories high, towered over the stone street, blocking the sun and causing the cascading water of the Thames to echo off the high walls. Merchants loudly hawked their wares from the thresholds of their shops as small children ran about, looking for pockets to pick. For a moment, Will thought to hold his money sack close; then he remembered he no longer had money nor a sack to put it in. Gone were the days when he had to guard himself against these marauding little thieves.

When Will reached the center of the bridge, he marveled, as he always did, at the Chapel of St. Thomas Becket. The chapel's windows were thin and high, allowing plenty of light into the inner church. A spiral staircase led down to the undercroft, which opened to the Thames. But his thoughts were broken by a sudden cry from a crowd amassing next to the chapel. The group peered over the bridge, shouting and pointing, and Will hurried over to see what caused the commotion. Below the bridge, the waters of the Thames were rough and coursing, and a body was caught in a whirlpool of water, refuse, twigs, and pebbles. A woman, her dark hair obscuring her face, was sucked under the water and then flung out on the other side of the bridge. Will turned to the man next to him. "What happened?" he asked.

"I don't know," the man replied. "She came from there," he said, pointing to Southwark. "She just walked up to the edge and jumped off."

"She be a whore from the Cat," a stooped woman interjected. "Those Cat whores are always jumping into the river."

Will shook his head and walked away. The Cat was a notorious brothel employing the most desperate of people. Filled with disease, women either too old or too young to be plying the trade and boys who were equally as desperate, one could buy services there for a sixpence or less. The Thames was littered with employees of the Cat; it seemed at least once a week someone from there took the leap from the bridge.

Shaken, Will continued past the Chapel of St. Thomas Becket. Such a thing of beauty, Will thought. Yet he remained aware of the dead prostitute floating under the bridge and the traitors' heads on pikes that lined the gate leading to Southwark.

The Axe was not far from Drawbridge Gate, and Will, after crossing the bridge, hurried down the street that led to Topside's brothel. The deeper into Southwark Will went, the dirtier the alleys became. It took an effort to avoid discarded food, the contents of chamber pots, and dead roosters that had been on the losing end of the cockfights for which Southwark was famous.

Will finally reached the Axe. A young woman stood outside, leaning against the timber walls of the brothel, her low-cut dress dirty and askew, her hair matted in the back. "Will," she drawled. "It's been a while."

Will smiled at the prostitute. "Ivy," he said. "How's business?"

"Ah," she said, waving her hand at Will dismissively. "The same gents. The same cocks. Nothing changes." Ivy looked tired and worn. Under her cheap face powder, Ivy had dark circles under her puffy, bloodshot eyes.

Will patted Ivy on the shoulder as he walked up the three steps to the Axe. He noted one was broken, and his hopes raised somewhat. Perhaps he could make a shilling or two that afternoon. "Is Ellyn inside?" he asked.

"Yes, and she's in a right foul mood."

Will opened the door and entered the Axe. The air was full of a powdery, heady smell - sex and cheap perfume mixed with lye. Ellyn prided herself on keeping an unsullied brothel.

Ellyn stood in a corner, arguing with a short man. "My girls are *clean*," she said, poking a stubby finger at the man's chest. "You

THE FAILED APPRENTICE

didn't get the pox from here. And next time you make such an accusation, you'll leave here without your balls."

The man's eyes widened. He looked at Will, turned, and hurried out of the brothel. "Bastard," Ellyn said, looking at Will. "That arse dared tell me one of my girls gave him the clap." She laughed. "It may be true, but he best not be telling me about it."

"I doubt you'll see him again," Will said. "He couldn't get out of here fast enough." Then: "You heard about Topside?"

"I did. He was a greedy one. It was only a matter of time. No great loss, for me anyway."

Will sighed. "Yet it is for me. He did not pay his guild dues. I am out of an apprenticeship." Will looked at the floor, covered in rushes that clearly needed changing. "I've come to see if you have any work for me."

Ellyn raised an eyebrow. "*Any* work?"

Will was momentarily taken aback. He coughed. "I was talking about repairs," he finally croaked. "I see you have a broken step in the front. I can fix it for a price."

"Ah, a shame," Ellyn said. "I could fetch some good coins for you."

Will felt heat creeping up his face and reddening his cheeks. "Thanks, but I'm not interested."

"Very well. Yes, you can do some repairs. There's the step outside and a hole in one of the upstairs walls. Fist-sized. I'll pay you a shilling."

Will nodded. "I'll get right to work."

Ellyn kept the supplies necessary for the smooth running of the Axe in the building's damp, dark basement. The steps down were rickety, and Will made a mental note to repair those as well. He started, though, with the steps leading to the Axe. Once outside, he looked around, but Ivy was no longer lingering by the door. Perhaps she had enticed a man to come inside, or perhaps she had had enough of the life of a bawdy girl and walked away. Will hoped that walk did not lead her to the Thames.

Repairing the step was easy, as was the hole in the wall in one of the upstairs rooms. Sunlight was beginning to wane as Will returned his supplies to the basement and approached Ellyn. "Done," he said. "Although this place could use some more work."

Ellyn nodded and handed Will a shilling. "Come back tomorrow," she said. "We've had a few wealthy mutton mongers visit us lately. They seem quite taken with our ladies." She jangled her coin purse. "We may have to fancy this place up!"

Will pocketed the shilling and smiled. "I am at your service, Ellyn," he said. "With Topside gone, there's no longer a middleman. More profits for you."

The sun was setting as Will hurried through the darkening streets of Southwark and to London Bridge. As he passed Drawbridge Gate, the ambient light of the setting sun flickered off the traitors' heads, illuminating bone and blackened sinew; Will glanced away and quickened his pace. Church bells would be tolling soon, marking the end of the day and the locking of London's gates. He did not want to be caught in Southwark, staring at the heads of men who had met such ignoble ends.

Will arrived home just as Elizabeth was lighting tallow candles on the trestle table. Once again, a thin cabbage pottage was served in small wooden bowls, and Will's brothers were hitting each other with spoons. Peter stood with his back to the door, starting at the fireplace full of ashes and a charred piece of wood.

"Here," Will said, approaching his father. "I have work. I don't expect you to support me."

Peter turned and looked at Will holding out the shilling. "Where did this come from?"

Will rehearsed what he would say if his father posed such a question all the way back from Southwark. "A friend of Topside's," he began, carefully maintaining eye contact with Peter. "He found me some work." Not a lie completely, just not the entire truth.

Peter took the shilling. "Regular work?" he asked.

Will looked his father in the eye. "Regular work," he said, trying to believe his own words.

THE FAILED APPRENTICE

Chapter 4

Will returned to the Axe the following day. He was relieved to see Ivy back outside, although she still looked tired and haggard. Will nodded to her as he climbed the steps to the brothel, noticing his handiwork as he reached the door. The stairs he had fixed the day before looked almost new.

Ellyn was sitting in a worn armchair in the center of the room, fanning herself with a dirty piece of paper. "Will," she said, smiling and showing a mouth containing only a few blackened teeth. "I'm glad you're back. A couple of the upstairs rooms need some attention. There's a hole in the floor in one and a cracked door leading to another. When you're done, I'm thinking of whitewashing the walls."

Will looked around the room. The casement windows were thrown open, letting in light and air - and the heavy smells of Southwark. But at least a breeze flowed through the room, dissipating the humidity and smell of close bodies. The Axe's front room was worn; the few chairs were covered in fabric, but the cloth was frayed and stained. If Ellyn wanted to add class to the Axe, she had a lot of work to do.

"What are you standing around for?" Ellyn said, interrupting Will's thoughts. "You best get working. I'm expecting some important clients this afternoon. I can't have your banging interrupting their banging." Ellyn chuckled at her joke.

Will could only imagine who Ellyn deemed important. The Axe was not known for attracting high class clientele. Although not as disreputable as the Cat, the Axe serviced a middling group of men. Not scoundrels, for the most part, but not part of London's elite either.

Will went about his repairs. After fixing the door to one of the upstairs rooms, he began work on the hole in the floor. As church bells heralded noon, he heard some conversation from below. The voices were raised, angry.

"You think you're so high and mighty, Ellyn," a man's voice barked, a sinister edge defining it. "You best watch it, or what happened to Topside might happen to you."

Ellyn raised her voice, drowning out the man. "Topside got whacked because he was skimming. I'm not skimming. You'll get your money, what you been promised, fair and square."

There was a pause in the conversation, and Will crept closer to the staircase. Skimming, so that was it - that's what caused Topside's death and the destruction of his home and forge. Topside was taking a larger cut of Axe profits than he was permitted, denying the Bishop of Winchester his rightful due. Will should have guessed. "You see I get what's mine," the man continued, clearly menacing. "I know you have Richard Rich and his ilk coming here. I know you're overcharging them, which is fine as long as I get my share."

"*Your* share? Don't you mean the Bishops share? You'll get the money, don't you worry," Ellyn growled. "Just get your fat arse out of my place of business." Will heard a slap, a cry, then a door opening and slamming shut.

Will rushed down the stairs to see Ellyn holding her shoulder. She looked at Will. "That churl hit me in the shoulder," she said. "Don't he know you don't hit a lady?"

"Who was that?" Will asked, staring at the door, which had been knocked off one of its hinges.

"Just one of Winchester's men," Ellyn sadly laughed. "Religious men, they pack a punch. I don't think the Bishop knows what a brute his courier is. Come to collect his "taxes." Now that Topside is dead, he thinks he can come right to me, that I don't recognize cheating when I see it."

"Are you all right?" Will asked.

"Oh, this?" Ellyn continued to rub her shoulder. "This is nothing. I got stubbed toes worse than this. But next time that churl comes poking around here, I'll have my dirk ready."

Will did not like the turn the conversation was taking. "I best repair that door," he said, motioning to the door hanging askew.

"Get on it," Ellyn said.

THE FAILED APPRENTICE

Fixing the door did not take much effort, and Will finished it and returned to put the final touches on the repairs he made to the floor. As he gathered his tools, he heard conversation from the front room. Yet, unlike Winchester's man, these voices were hushed and refined. Will walked down the staircase to see Ellyn surrounded by two gentlemen, one fair and one dark, dressed in woolen finery. Each wore long gowns over their jerkins and hose. From the material alone, Will knew they were men of wealth.

Will hung back as Ellyn talked price with the duo. "I want the same strumpet I had last time," the fairer one said, winking at Ellyn. "She gave my cock a good ride!"

His friend glanced at Will. "Is he available?" The second man said, a hopeful lilt in his voice.

Will blanched. "Oh, no, that's just Will," Ellyn said. "He does repairs for me."

"A shame," the man said. "But no mind. I'll take whoever you got, preferably a redhead."

"I'll be outside," Will mouthed to Ellyn, anxious to get away from the men.

Minutes later, Ellyn emerged from the Axe. "Here's two shillings, Will," she said. "One for your work and one for keeping your mouth shut from what you have seen in here today."

Will nodded, pocketing the coins. "I didn't see a thing."

Ellyn nodded. "Come back tomorrow. The smaller one is hard on the rooms," she said as she turned and walked back inside.

Will headed back to London Bridge. So far, he had earned three shillings by working for Ellyn. A skilled tradesman could make that in a week; Will managed to do so in two days. Not bad for a failed apprentice.

That night Will gave his father one of his two shillings. The other he kept in a small leather sack under his pallet. He had three solid days of work behind him. Why shouldn't he keep some of his wages?

Chapter 5

Working at the Axe proved fortuitous for Will. Ellyn was correct when she said her new clientele was hard on the house. Over the course of a week, Will repaired two doors, the staircase banister, two bed frames, and the side wall of the privy hidden behind the house. Every day he left with two or three shillings in his pocket, and he always handed one over to his father. The others he added to his small sack. Every night he weighed the bag in his hand. Bit by bit, it was getting heavier, the coins musically clinking together.

A week passed, and Will was heading home from the Axe. He was feeling pretty good about himself; he had managed to squirrel away five shillings and a few pence in the bag under his mattress. He gave the remainder to his father. Peter never asked for the details of what kind of work Will was doing. Will assumed his father thought he was smithing, but something in Peter's eyes told Will he was happy not to know the logistics of Will's employ.

That afternoon Will took his time crossing the bridge. He barely glanced at the traitors' heads and meandered toward the Chapel of St. Thomas Becket, marveling at the shops and homes that flanked the cobbled road and the wide-wheeled carriages that lumbered down the street. He stopped to gaze into a shop that sold men's cloth, imagining himself in a doublet with slit arms, like he had seen Ellyn's new, wealthy clients wearing. Because of Henry VIII's sumptuary laws, Will knew he could not wear imported wool or fur and various colors, including gold, silver, and purple. Wearing satin, velvet, and damask was also forbidden for one of his class. Despite Peter's good reputation, the Pattens were not of high enough rank, nor rich enough, nor noble enough to allow for such items. One day, though, Will thought, imagining himself in a cloak lined with ermine, a doublet with slit satin sleeves.

An insistent nudge at his elbow pulled Will from his reverie. His hand went to his small bag, where his two shillings were stuck

THE FAILED APPRENTICE

together. "Calm down, Will. I'm not here to rob you," a woman's voice chided. "But if you have any extra coins, I'd be much obliged."

Will turned and was surprised to see his sister Amy smiling at him. "I saw you walk past," she continued. "I live right there." Amy pointed to a large, three-story home, the back of it hanging precipitously over the Thames.

Will embraced Amy, feeling the coarse fabric of her gown against his rough hands. Then he stepped back and looked at his sister. Amy and Will looked alike, both were tall, thin, with blond hair and sharp gray eyes. Amy had filled out since Will had seen her last, yet the vestige of a girl remained in her trusting face. "Amy, I'm so happy to see you," he exclaimed.

"You too, Will," Amy said, surveying her brother. "You look good. Still skinny, but good!"

Will smiled. He had put on weight since working at the Axe but was still lanky. "Do you like it?" he said, cocking his head toward the house. "Being a domestic?"

The two moved over to the side of the road, out of the way of carriages and people rushing across the bridge. "It's all right," Amy said. "The mistress is nice. The master is a bit off, but the work is not too hard. Yet I don't think it's the right job for me. I don't see the dust and dirt, then I'm reprimanded for not cleaning it up."

Will took Amy's hands in his. Normally soft, her long fingers and palms had developed cracks and callouses. "Will, stop," she said, noticing the sad look sweeping over his face. "It's fine. Nothing I can't handle." She pulled her hands away. "And you? Why aren't you at the forge?"

Obviously, Amy had not heard about Topside's untimely end. He told her about the men, the splash of the body as it hit the Thames, the destruction of the forge. "I'm working at the Axe," he said. "Fixing things. I'm making money."

"The Axe?" Amy said, her eyes widening. "I hope our parents don't know about this; they'd have a fit."

Will laughed. "They think I'm working for a friend of Topside's, which I am, in a way."

The door to Amy's house opened, and an older woman in a white bonnet peered out. "Amy, the mistress is looking for you," the woman called. "You best get your hide inside!"

Amy gave Will a quick hug. "I'll be looking for you when you cross the bridge," she said hurriedly. "I'll come out if I can."

Will watched Amy disappear into the house. It was a fine home with mullioned windows, a tiled roof, fresh whitewash, and new timbers. It was much nicer than the Pattens' small, worn home. It was the type of home Amy should be living in, if only as a domestic.

For the next several weeks, Will found steady employment at the Axe. Ellyn's new, wealthy patrons brought their friends, and the brothel's reputation rose. Ellyn's prices also increased, and Will was rewarded in kind. As London's summer heat abated and was replaced by the cool breezes of autumn, Will was confident that Topside's untimely passing had been a blessing in disguise.

In November, Ellyn pulled Will aside. "Take this sack," she said, holding out a large leather bag filled with coins. "It's for the new bishop. He sent word that the old courier died, probably from being an arsehole," she laughed. "The new man will meet you outside the palace. Probably thinks he's too good to enter the Stews."

The Stews were the name given to the brothels of Southwark. Most likely originating from the term "stew ponds," the area where the Bishop of Winchester had once bred fish, the Stews had since become synonymous with Southwark's most notorious form of entertainment. Will nodded and took the bag, securing it under his cloak. Traveling to the palace was a short, easy walk, and Will would enjoy getting away from the Axe for a while.

Will made his way eastward, down Bankend, to the palace. The area surrounding the Axe was populated with other brothels; women lounged on stoops, their faces caked with hastily applied rouge and lipstick. Several called to Will, offering their services. Will ignored them and moved on. Although the walk to the palace

THE FAILED APPRENTICE

was short, several men, their clothes torn and stained, watched him with interest. Will became conscious of the sack of coins under his cloak, attached to his belt, bouncing off his thigh with every step. He knew he was an easy target he was for thieves and felt his heart begin to race.

Yet Will soon arrived at the palace with his coin pouch intact. Winchester Palace was large, with heavy stonework and long windows secured with plate tracery. The smell of roasting meat wafted from the palace's nearby kitchens. An immense rose window towered over the crowded, grimy streets. Will marveled at how close the palace was to the poverty of Southwark - the decrepit houses, the illicit brothels, the blood sports of cock fighting and bear baiting. Wealth and power so close to the dirty and powerless, who lived just a stone's throw away.

After a short wait, a man close to Will's age approached him, although his fur-lined cape attested to him moving in very different social circles. "Are you Will?" he asked. The man's face was deeply scarred; he had obviously been a victim of smallpox. At least he had survived the deadly disease.

"I'm Will," Will said, trying to avert his eyes from the pox scars.

"I'm Nick Greene," the man said. "Bishop Gardiner's man. I believe you have something for me?"

Will produced the bag of coins. "It's all there," he said.

Nick smiled. "I have no doubt. You know the penalties for theft. Especially theft from the bishop." Nick's eyes bulged in mock terror.

Will nodded. "I am aware."

"Thank you for the safe delivery," Nick said. "Bishop Gardiner will be glad of it."

Will was rarely thanked for any of his efforts. Topside did little more than grunt when Will accomplished anything at the forge, and Ellyn just piled more requests upon Will when he had repaired a stair or filled in a hole. And his parents - they were too busy trying to merely survive than note any of Will's contributions. He wasn't sure how to respond to this clearly wealthy man who looked at Will and smiled.

"You are welcome," Will stammered.

Nick nodded. "I'm sure we will see more of each other," he said as he turned and disappeared through the heavy palace doors.

The sun was beginning its descent, and Will had finished his work for the day. London Bridge was in sight, and Will decided to go directly home. A cold wind blew as Will crossed the bridge and turned west onto Thames Street, hugging his cloak next to his body, glad to not feel the thud of a heavy money pouch against his leg. Suddenly, a swell of people surrounded Will, their yells raucous and loud. Fearing being trampled, Will moved to the side of the road. Moments later, three horses came into view. The riders, however, sat backward, overlooking the horses' tails. The mob continued to jeer and pelt the riders with rotting fruit and feces - both animal and human. As the horses passed, Will saw that the riders had paper attached to their clothes. Two riders looked down, shame lining their faces, but a third looked at the crowd, defiant. He caught Will's eye and spat. Will struggled to see what was attached to his shirt, but between the angry mob and the rapidity with which the horses passed, he could see little, just dark writing on stained paper.

After the throng passed, an older man turned to Will, a piece of rotten apple still clinging to his cloak, and shook his head. "I've never seen that before. Heretics on display."

"Heretics?" Will said, confused.

"They were caught with banned books. Heretical texts. Parts of the text were pinned to their clothes. They'll travel like this to the cross at Cheapside. Lord Chancellor Thomas More came up with this punishment as a lesson to other apostates. These men got lucky; More is fond of burning heretics."

Will and the man moved down the road where the horses had passed moments before, carefully avoiding the fruit and dung littering the street. "I fear there will be more deaths. In fact, I am sure of it. The church is heading toward a crisis."

THE FAILED APPRENTICE

Will looked questioningly at the man. Will, like all of England, was Catholic. Although not as religious as many men his age, Will had grown up believing in the absoluteness of the church. To hear it was in crisis was unfathomable. "I cannot imagine that," he said.

"It's the king. He is intent on divorce," the man lowered his voice. "Queen Katherine has been moved from the royal residence to Herefordshire. The king doesn't want to see her, and there are rumors he is in love with someone at court. Someone he intends to marry. The Pope will not grant the king the divorce he desires. England is heading toward war with Rome, and I fear more men will meet the flame or the sword." He looked around nervously. "But you didn't hear that from me."

For once, Will was glad of his lowly status. No one cared what he believed or thought. He wasn't worth the kindling it would take to start a fire under his feet.

Will and the older man parted at Suffolk Lane. Their short conversation was Will's first glimpse of a world outside the forge, his family's crowded household, or the Axe. And it was a dangerous world at that.

When Will arrived at the Axe the next morning, Ellyn was outside arguing with a round, red-faced man who leaned menacingly toward her. "I demand my money back," the man yelled, standing a bit straighter but still not as tall as Ellyn.

"Surely there wasn't a problem," Ellyn said, her eyes narrowing, her voice laced with anger.

"Yes, there was indeed a problem," the man said. "Your girl was rude to me. Said my cock looked like a dung beetle." He pulled back and adjusted his dark wool breeches. "I will not stand for that."

Ellyn stifled a laugh but met the man's eye. "There be no refunds."

Will looked more closely at the man. He was middle-aged, and his clothing was expensive; Will guessed he was part of the growing merchant class that was gaining wealth all over London. Tufts of black hair stood up in sections on his head, with a swathe combed back to cover a bald spot. He looked at Will, nostrils flaring. "What are you looking at, cur?" he spat. Will averted his eyes.

Stepping back, Ellyn appraised the man. Will could almost hear her thoughts. He was clearly rich and, if treated well, would return and perhaps bring more wealthy friends. "Very well," she sighed, reaching into the small purse hanging from her waist and extracting several shillings. "That is an insult not warranted. I will speak to the girl and guarantee that behavior will not be repeated."

The man took the shillings and smiled smugly. "Very well," he said. "I will be back. But next time, I expect a girl who appreciates my more than ample gifts." He thrust his hips slightly toward Ellyn.

Will and Ellyn watched the man turn to leave. "That was Hugh Culler, a merchant, new money. Sometimes I prefer the rabble who used to come here," she said. "All these rich men act like they be owed something."

THE FAILED APPRENTICE

Chapter 6

Two weeks later, Will made his way home across the bridge. It was getting dark earlier, and the wind whipped down the street, causing Will to pull his thin cloak tighter around his body. The casual camaraderie of people shopping that summer had been replaced by those hurrying through the cold, eyes downcast, breath escaping in misty bursts.

Halfway across the bridge, Will passed the towering gables of Amy's house. He stopped for a moment and thought Amy lucky; she was able to live in a fine home with a warm bedroom and good food, not like his experience with Topside or his work at the Axe. Sighing, he looked up and was surprised to see Amy peering out of one of the upper windows. Amy stood immobile, staring into space yet seeing nothing. Even from a distance, Will noticed a sadness about her. He raised his hand in greeting.

Moments later, Amy looked down and noticed Will watching her. A slow smile spread across her face. She held up a finger for Will to wait.

Will stood, hopping from one foot to the other to keep warm. Eventually, the door slowly opened, and Amy eased out. Although she smiled, Will was shocked at the change in his sister. Her skin, normally lustrous, was pale and dull, her eyes worn and empty. She had lost weight, and her lips were dry and cracked, a trace of blood visible at the corner of her mouth. "Oh my God, Amy," Will said, eyes widening.

"I know I look a wreck," Amy said, smoothing her apron, which was spotted with grease. She tried to laugh, but the sound was hollow.

"Are they mistreating you?" Will asked, panic rising in his voice. "Because that was surely not the agreement when they took you on."

Amy coughed. "I am fine, Will. It's just hard work."

"I know what hard work looks like, Amy. And this is not it."

Amy glanced behind her. "The master. He can be," she searched for the right word. "Difficult. And a bit too interested in the help."

Will shut his eyes, trying to block out the image. "He better not have laid a finger on you," Will said. "Or he will deal with me."

"Will, you are not nearly as fearsome as you think you are," Amy said. "Anyway, I am good at avoiding him. Some of the girls aren't as fortunate. But I know when to make myself scarce."

"Do you have a friend in the house? Someone who can look out for you?"

Amy shook her head, her eyes glistening with unshed tears. "I did, but she is gone," she said, glancing behind her at the doorway, the stoop covered in a light dusting of snow. "I best get back inside."

Will grabbed Amy's arm as she turned to go, feeling the boniness of it through her thin cloak. "You come and find me at the Axe if things get bad," he said. "Promise me."

Amy looked at him and nodded. "I promise."

Will was oblivious to the cold as he trudged back to Fenn Road. The change in Amy was so marked, so dramatic, that he was certain things were much worse than she implied. Surely his father would not stand for his eldest daughter being mistreated. Will was so lost in thought that he almost passed his home in the falling darkness of the evening.

The warm blast from the fire in the Pattens' hearth was welcome after the cold walk and the chilling sight of his sister. Lately, fortune had smiled upon Will. His contributions to the household were evident: a fire roared in the hearth and fresh rushes, interspersed with dried rosemary stems, lined the floor. For years rushes were considered an unnecessary luxury, and the family became used to the packed earth floor. But the Pattens' lifestyle had improved in these small ways now that Will was contributing to the family income.

"Will, come sit," Elizabeth said, motioning to his place at the table. "I made a stew. With meat." Will smiled. Another luxury. His brothers were already finishing the contents of their bowls and had begun banging them on the table.

THE FAILED APPRENTICE

Will sat next to his father and ate his meal in silence. When he had finished, he turned to Peter. "I am worried," he said. "Worried about Amy."

"Amy?" Elizabeth said, her head snapping up.

"When have you seen Amy?" Peter asked, pushing back from the table.

Will knew he had to tread carefully. Any mention of crossing the bridge to and from Southwark would raise suspicions. "I was sent on an errand," he said. "To buy some materials from a shop on the bridge. I saw Amy there, outside her master's house."

Fortunately, his parents were more concerned about Amy than what Will was doing on the bridge. "And?" Peter prodded.

"She looked awful. Drawn, tired."

"It's no surprise. I am sure domestic work has been difficult for her," Peter said.

"It's not just that," Will continued, glancing at his brothers and lowering his voice. "She implied that the master of the house has," Will hesitated. "Made advances."

Elizabeth sighed and looked at her hands, but it was Peter who spoke up. "She must learn to deal with that," he said. "It's an age-old problem."

"I don't think you understand," Will persisted. "Her master is a lecher."

Peter hesitated. "We understand, Will. And there's nothing to be done. Domestic work is an honorable profession, and Amy is lucky to be working in a fine home. She must learn how to handle such men. I'm sure this won't be the first time she will deal with this. Or the last."

Will looked at Elizabeth, hoping for help. Instead, she smiled sadly. "Your father is right, Will. Best you stay out of it."

Will was stunned. Surely they did not understand the untenable position in which Amy found herself. "But this man, he has…."

Peter cut him off. "What would you have us do, Will? Remove her from service? Then what?"

Will looked around. His family was just starting to climb out of poverty, and Peter would not welcome Amy back home, another mouth to feed, another body to clothe. In his father's eyes, he had failed as a blacksmith; he would not welcome another of his children failing in their work. Will said nothing.

"The Cullers are a respected family. Up and coming in London," Peter continued. "Hugh Culler is a prosperous merchant. If Amy is smart, she can stick with this family all the way to a fine mansion on the Strand or even a country estate."

Culler? That was the name of the man who had given Ellyn such a difficult time at the Axe. So now Will could put a face to the man harassing his sister. He would not forget.

When Will returned to the Axe the following day, he asked Ellyn about Culler. "Aye, he's been back," she said. "Always haggling me for a lower price. "This girl said that," he says. Or "this girl did that." Since that one time, though, I make him cough up what's due."

"Let me know when he returns," Will said.

Ellyn looked at him, her eyes narrowing. "You got a problem with him?"

"No problem," Will lied.

Ellyn continued to look at him. "Well, all right," she finally said. "Since you're here, I have money for the Bishop. You can meet his man at the Tower."

"The Tower?" Will asked. "The palace is so close. Why the Tower?"

"You're asking me?" Ellyn said. "I just do as I'm told."

Ellyn handed Will the heavy money sack. Its weight had increased since the last time Will met Nick. Will jostled the bag and smiled. "Them rich ones, they pay," Ellyn said. "And you best keep those coins well hidden."

Will put the bag in his cloak, once again feeling the weight settle against his thigh. "I'll keep it safe," he said. Then, as an afterthought, "Just let me know when Culler comes back."

The walk across the bridge was cold, but Will stopped and lingered outside Amy's house. He searched the windows but saw no sign of life. Eventually, he moved on, clutching the money bag under his cloak, tight against his body.

THE FAILED APPRENTICE

Will's heart skipped a beat when the Tower of London came into view. Its white stone walls, heavy and impenetrable, loomed over the Thames and were a powerful reminder of the strength of the Crown. Will had heard that some prisoners - usually important ones - arrived at the Tower through St. Thomas' Tower, a dark, secretive gate accessible only via the Thames. Lesser prisoners were ushered in through the front entrance, where Will was to meet the bishop's liaison.

Will lingered in front of the gate, tapping down the fear that he would be mistaken for an escaped prisoner and pulled into one of the Tower's dark cells. He moved away from the iron gates, nodding to the yeoman warders who guarded the Tower, and stood underneath a nearby yew tree.

Nick arrived shortly after Will and greeted him with a smile and a pat on the back. Will was glad to see Nick and pass the money sack to him; thankfully, he had managed to transport it without it being stolen or lost. He opened his cloak and handed Nick the worn leather bag. "A good haul," Nick said, weighing the bag in his hand appreciatively before attaching it to his thick leather belt, hidden safely beneath his cape. "Let me run the money inside and give it to the bishop; you stay here." Nick turned and disappeared through the Tower gates.

Nick returned moments later. "The money's been delivered," he said. "Bishop Gardiner thanks you. But now I have to go to Smithfield to represent him. Come with me, I could use the company. We'll catch a wherry."

Will was in no hurry to return to the Axe. He and Nick walked toward the Thames and picked up a wherry at Watergate, Nick offering the wherryman a coin for the ride. Will took a seat near the pointed bow of the small wooden boat while Nick sat to the side. As they traveled down the Thames toward Smithfield, Will thought of George Topside floating among the debris, bobbing lifelessly in the cold river. Bodies were regularly pulled from the Thames, and Will cringed when he thought of the ones that remained unfound, bones settling in the muck at the bottom of the black river, mud coating the remains of those who met untimely deaths and would be soon forgotten.

Will and Nick disembarked at Blackfriar's and began the short walk down Old Bailey Street to Smithfield. Passing Newgate Prison, the cries of those inside the prison's stone walls broke through the noise of the crowd heading toward Smithfield. "Newgate," Nick said, shaking his head. "What a hellhole. I sure wouldn't want to be in there."

Will had heard horror stories about the prison, chiefly from Topside, who passed them along to Will with relish. Although most prisoners were impoverished, they were expected to pay for their own food and bedding. Lice, bedbugs, and vermin were so profuse that crossing the floor often resulted in a sickening crunching. Before meeting their fate on the gallows, many prisoners died from gaol fever, victims of the infectious diseases that raged through the prison. Some corpses remained shackled to the walls days after their deaths, the jailers either too busy or too lazy to remove the bodies.

Will sighed in relief as they finally passed the prison, although entering Smithfield filled him with a new sense of horror. A platform had been erected in the center of the square, piles of wood placed below a towering stake. Will turned to Nick. "Tell me there will not be a burning here today."

"There will be," Nick said. "That's why I'm here, representing Bishop Gardiner. One of the downsides to my job."

"I wish you'd have told me that's why we were coming," Will said. "I would have gladly returned to the Axe."

"Well, now you're here," Nick said. "Have you ever seen a burning? It's quite a gruesome spectacle."

"Never," Will said. "And I don't want to start today." He looked at Nick, who shrugged his shoulders. Will understood he was there for the duration.

Crowds were already amassed around the pyre. Women of all ages stood together, their gowns ranging from rags to finely woven cloth. Some were hawking their wares - cheaply made handkerchiefs that could be dipped in the blood of the condemned for good luck. There would be no hanging, drawing, and quartering today, nor a simple beheading - Will assumed the women were looking ahead to future opportunities. Meanwhile, children chased each other through the crowd, and men stood together, laughing, casting eyes toward Newgate, anticipating the prisoner's arrival.

"Who is it?" Will asked, his stomach sinking, knowing he could not leave. "Who is to be burned?"

"Richard Bayfield. An educated man, a former Benedictine monk. He's been circulating all sorts of heretical texts, including the works of Luther."

Will's shoulders slumped. He had no idea who Luther was.

Nick moved closer to Will and lowered his voice. "If you ask me, death will be a relief for Bayfield. He has been chained, tortured, and beaten to make him recant his heresies. The beatings were so severe that Bayfield has barely any flesh left on his back. Yet after all this, he refused to recant." Nick shook his head, then added, "More is making an example of him," nodding at a man sitting on a raised dais above the crowd.

So that's Sir Thomas More, Will thought, Lord Chancellor to King Henry. He surveyed the man, dressed in heavy furs, protecting himself against the biting cold. His chain of office hung prominently across his chest, the metal glinting in the cold sunlight. More was older than Will imagined; he must be in his early fifties. Although he was seated, Will could see More was not tall, yet he projected power even from a distance. More's face, pale and severe, regarded the growing crowd. He smiled as the square filled, bodies pressing together, jockeying for a spot near the pyre.

Moments later, a roar rose from the mob. An old man appeared, worn, exhausted, and beaten. Two guards dragged him through the jeering crowd to the stake, where a heavy chain encircled him several times, securing him to the post. Bayfield looked not at the mob but heavenward, his tremulous voice surprisingly strong, rising in prayer.

Will turned away as the pyre was lit. His eyes fastened on an older woman, her dress in tatters, screaming "heretic!" Will wondered if she even knew what the word meant.

Fifteen minutes later, the fire was still going, and Bayfield was still alive, low moans escaping above the crackling of the wood. The kindling had been damp and burned slowly, either by design or accident. As Will looked at More, whose eyes had not left Bayfield since the fire was lit, he became convinced that the slow, torturous death was part of More's plan.

Another fifteen minutes passed, and Bayfield still lived. Will did not think this possible. The man had been chained to the pyre for close to thirty minutes, the fire slowly licking his gown, the smoldering ashes rising and burning his lungs. But the fire was not hot enough, nor the smoke thick enough, to be fatal. Eventually, the fabric covering Bayfield's left arm caught fire, and he reached with his right hand to extinguish the blaze. The sudden movement caused the incinerated arm to completely fall off. After that, it was not long until Bayfield took his last breath.

"Well, that's done," Nick said. "Took a lot longer than I thought. I've done my duty. Gardiner will be happy. I hope that's the last one of these I have to see for a while."

The crowd began to disperse. Will glanced at More, who had climbed down from the dais and approached the pyre, the chains now hanging limply against the stake, Bayfield's bones now a smoldering pile amongst the unburnt wood. Will put his hand on Nick's arm and nodded toward More, who was stomping on what little was left of Bayfield. "I don't understand the hatred," Will said.

"I don't either," Nick replied. "But it's not our job to. Our job is to keep our heads down and survive."

The two walked back down Old Bailey Street toward the wherries. "Do you have time for an ale?" Nick asked. "I could use a drink after that."

"I do," Will said. Breathing the acrid smoke had left him parched.

THE FAILED APPRENTICE

Will and Nick found a nearby tavern, the interior dark but with a roaring fire which cast flickering shadows upon the walls. They sat at a table near the blaze, the fire warming and comforting, unlike the flames that had taken Bayfield's life and destroyed Topside's forge.

Tankards of ale were ordered, and Will began to relax in the warmth of the tavern. Nick took a deep pull on his ale and spoke. "What is your story, Will? You don't seem the type to be working at a brothel."

Will relayed his tale of woe - from his less than satisfactory experience with Topside to the burning of Topside's home and forge to his frustrating experience with the guild. "I had little choice," he said. "My family can barely make ends meet as it is. I needed to earn some money. The Axe seemed the only option at the time."

Nick nodded. "You are educated; that is clear," he said.

"I learned to read and write when I was young," Will replied. "When my parents had time to teach me. I'm afraid my younger brothers and baby sister won't be as lucky."

"You are wasting your talents at the Axe," Nick said.

"What choice do I have?" Will peered into his now empty tankard. He knew Nick was right. His career at the Axe would not suffice for the long haul. "I know it's not ideal."

"Keep your eyes open. I will too. There's always a place for a smart, ambitious young man. I have seen stranger things than men rise from nothing to positions of power."

"Power!" Will laughed. "I'd just be happy to make an honest living."

Nick smiled, and Will realized, not for the first time, how much he had missed the companionship of a friend.

"Now let me ask you something," Will said, then paused. A germ of fear had been building in his gut since the burning had begun. There was a frightening undercurrent sweeping through London, and Will wanted to be sure he didn't get caught up in it. "Who is Luther?" he asked. If following Luther could get you incinerated, he'd like to know who the man was.

Nick sighed. "Luther is a German who is very critical of the church. He believes many things - heretical things - ideas in opposition to Rome. He thinks everyone should be able to read the Bible, not just priests. He doesn't believe in transubstantiation."

"The Eucharist?" Will said, incredulous. Turning bread and wine into Christ's body and blood was the cornerstone of the Catholic Church.

Nick nodded. "All that and more. That's why Thomas More hates Luther and those like him. They're intent on stripping the church of its power. Another man in More's sights is William Tyndale, a bloke whose intent on translating the Bible into English, so everyone can read it. These are dangerous men, Will. You best not even utter their names."

So Will had his answer. The church's fear of losing power was behind this. He would keep that in mind.

The day was nearing an end as Will and Nick left the tavern and boarded a wherry at Blackfriars. "Did you see the burning?' the wherry operator asked as he pulled away from the quay. "Bet it was a good show. Did he light up like a torch?"

"It was a slow burn," Nick replied, turning his back to the wherryman, not wanting to engage him further.

The wherryman nodded and smiled. "Sorry I missed it. I like to see them heretics burn."

The sun was setting as Will and Nick disembarked at Watergate. He would not be returning to the Axe that day. He was sick of sweaty bodies and the smell of burned flesh; all he wanted to do was go home and crawl onto his pallet.

THE FAILED APPRENTICE

Chapter 7

December was uncharacteristically cold for London. The money Will brought in from the Axe went to purchasing firewood that kept the Pattens' small home warm and meat that made their meals hearty, if not of high quality. And the small sack hidden under his pallet also grew. Will had close to £2 by the middle of December, enough to feel his future was a bit more secure.

Although winter was usually a slow time at the Axe, December proved unusually busy. Ellyn's customers were now almost exclusively wealthier Londoners, her increasing prices forcing her old regulars to go elsewhere. The influx of new clients kept Will employed. Barely a day went by when there wasn't a stair that needed repair, a hole that needed boarding up, a wall that needed fresh paint.

One day in mid-December, Will was working on the stairway railing, which had developed a dangerous wobble. A frigid gust of wind startled him as the door blew open. A short man wrapped in a velvet, fur-lined cloak scurried in, slamming the door behind him. He looked around and pulled back his hood, exposing his short-cropped black hair. "Ellyn!" his voice boomed.

Will put down his tools and stood up. He recognized the man as Culler, Amy's master. This was affirmed when Ellyn ran into the room, wiping her hands in her skirts. "Master Culler!" she said. "How lovely to see you!"

Culler threw off his cape, which landed on a worn chair. "I'm here for my girl!" he demanded.

"Avis!" Ellyn screeched. At that, Avis, a tiny woman with a perpetually startled look, entered the room. "Master Culler is here to see you."

Avis' eyes widened as she attempted a forced smile. "Master Culler," she said and curtseyed.

Culler said nothing but turned and pushed past Will, Avis skittering behind him. "I'll give you your money when I'm through," he called to Ellyn, ignoring a blatant breach of brothel protocol. Once he was out of sight, Ellyn shook her head. "What a louse," she said under her breath and returned to the back of the house.

Will was about to return to his work on the railing, but his eyes kept returning to Culler's discarded cloak. It lay haphazardly on the chair, half of it trailing onto the floor. Will approached the cape and ran his hand over the soft fur lining. A quick glance around the room confirmed that he was alone. Quickly, he picked up the cape and threw it over his shoulders. Although Will was taller and more slender than Culler, the cloak fit him well.

Will had never felt the luxury of soft fur against his skin. You would never be cold in something like this, he thought, running his hands over the heavy green wool of the cape, fingering the silver clasps at the neck and chest. This cape alone would be worth a year of his wages from Ellyn. At least.

Will took a few steps, marveling at the cape billowing around him. Then, turning, he felt something bounce off his thigh. Taking off the cape, he noticed a small silk pouch attached to the lining, the green of the silk matching the green of the wool. For a moment, Will considered his find; but just for a moment. From what Will had seen, Culler was a mean man, bordering on cruel. Will opened the pouch to reveal several coins nestled together.

The coins were shiny and looked new. There were several pence, a few shillings, and even a couple pounds. Would Culler miss a few coins? Probably not. Could Will justify relieving him of the weight of some of the coins? Probably so. He remembered Culler cheating Ellyn, the look on Amy's face and her pale, haunted eyes, the way Culler ordered Avis around. Then he removed three shillings and returned the cape to the chair.

Will resumed his work on the railing as Ellyn entered the room. She picked up the cloak, shook her head in disgust, folded it, and returned it to the chair. Will's stomach clenched. What if Culler discovered the missing coins and blamed Ellyn? The accusation from someone as powerful as Culler would be devastating. Will vowed to return the money to the pouch once Ellyn left the room.

THE FAILED APPRENTICE

But Ellyn never returned to the back of the house and spent the next fifteen minutes tidying up the small front room and stoking the fire. Soon, heavy footsteps resounded in the upstairs hall, and Culler emerged at the top of the staircase. He adjusted his breeches and clamored down the stairs, again shouldering past Will. He looked about the room for his cloak, spotted it on the chair, grabbed it, and reached for his money pouch.

Will held his breath. Perhaps he should just confess to the theft. He was not a criminal and wasn't sure what had come over him. Surely an honest confession would be better than being caught with the stolen coins? He opened his mouth to speak, but nothing came out. He snapped it shut.

Culler opened his money pouch and poured a few coins into his chubby, pale hand. His sausage-like index finger separated the coins - pence, shilling, pound. He extracted a pound from the small pile and returned the others to the pouch. "Here's a pound," he said, handing the coin to Ellyn. "I'd like my girl to be in finer clothes next time I come, as befitting my position."

Ellyn took the coin. "Yes, Master Culler, I will see to it," she said, gaping at the pound.

"See that you do," Culler said as he swung the cloak over his shoulders and fastened it with the silver clip at his neckline. He turned and swept out of the Axe, not looking back.

Will slowly exhaled. He had gotten away with it. Culler hadn't noticed the missing coins, clutched in Will's hand, growing sticky with perspiration.

The theft did not weigh on Will's mind as much as he expected. Culler's dismissiveness and arrogance erased some of the trepidation Will felt. And, if dark thoughts began to overcome him, all he had to do was remember Amy and the fragile state in which he had found her that day on the bridge. Yet as Will crossed London Bridge that evening, he ducked into the Chapel of St. Thomas Becket. As his eyes adjusted to the dark, he sought out the alms box, a heavy wooden box affixed to a pillar with a thick leather strap and iron clasps. Will opened his small money pouch, removed the three ill-begotten shillings, and slid one into the box through a slit in its top. He returned the other two to the sack. Perhaps the shilling would help one of London's many poor, providing a meal or shelter for a night. They certainly needed it more than Culler.

Work at the Axe remained steady throughout December, and Culler remained a frequent visitor, although Will never had access to Culler's coin bag again. Although Culler continued to dismiss Ellyn and treat Avis with disrespect, he paid for his services without complaint, and Avis was pleased to have clean, new clothes, which Culler insisted upon and paid for. As the year turned to 1532, Will had saved a tidy sum, and although work at the Axe was never assured, he was pleased to have a place to go every day despite his parents' creeping suspicions that he was not actually working for a blacksmith.

One cold January day, Will arrived at the Axe later than usual. He had overslept, and a steady snowfall caused the cobblestone streets to become slick, resulting in slow going. He entered the Axe and shook off the snow that coated his hair and cloak. The fire was blazing, casting warmth throughout the room. But as Will looked around, an unexplained chill passed through him. Something was amiss. Avis and Ivy stood next to the fire, whispering, their eyes cast down, unable to meet Will's.

Moments later, Ellyn rounded the corner, her lips pursed, a mug of hot caudle in her hands. Blood smeared her apron. "What is it?" Will asked, his heart starting to pound in his chest.

"Amy," Ellyn said, her voice flat. "She's upstairs."

Will's eyes widened. "Amy?" He turned and raced up the stairs two at a time.

Will found Amy huddled in a back room, barely larger than a closet, shaking on a stained, sheetless mattress and under a thin blanket. Her long blonde hair hung limply around her pale face; the part of her shift he could see was dirty and torn. Her eyes, ringed in dark circles, were red from crying. She had a cut under her eye and a swollen lip, which she touched unconsciously. "Will," she said, her voice barely a whisper.

THE FAILED APPRENTICE

"What happened?" Will said, a creeping horror overtaking him. He felt Ellyn moving behind him, the three people filling the small room. Ellyn pushed past Will and handed Amy the steaming mug of warm ale and spices.

"Nothing happened. I am fine," Amy replied, clutching the caudle, her fingers a deathly white.

"You are clearly not fine," Will replied.

"I just had to get away. I had nowhere to go."

"Culler," Ellyn volunteered. At the mention of his name, Amy began to weep.

"What did he do?" Will said, his voice hard.

Amy shook her head and turned away.

"As best I understand it," Ellyn volunteered, "he cornered her last night and forced himself on her. She fought back, bless her. But you know Culler. She was no match for him. She fled his house at first light."

"I'll kill him," Will said.

"Will, no," Amy said. "Just leave it be. I don't want to cause trouble for you. I was lucky to put him off as long as I did. I should have known this would happen. I should have been more careful."

"Don't you be blaming yourself, Amy," Ellyn said. "I've never liked that man. You was just trying to do your job; he had no right." Ellyn looked at Will and lowered her voice. "He's been roughing Avis up a bit. He will no longer be welcome here."

Will sat on the thin mattress next to Amy and touched her shoulder, but she recoiled. "Are you hurt?" he asked. Clearly, she was.

"I put salve on her cuts," Ellyn volunteered. "And she was bleeding. I think that's through, though." Amy nodded.

"I will fetch a doctor," Will said.

"No, please," Amy said, barely a whisper. "I'll be fine. But I can't go back. I can't face that man."

The sound of a slamming door from below caused all three to look up, startled. "You stay here as long as you need to," Ellyn said as she turned to attend to whoever had just entered the Axe. "Me and Will, we're like family. I take care of my own."

Will looked at Ellyn's retreating form and raised an eyebrow at Amy. Family?

"What if that's Culler?" Amy said, ignoring Ellyn's familial pronouncement. "What if he's come for me?"

"If it's Culler, I *will* kill him."

Amy shook her head. "You are not helping, Will. What am I going to do? I can't stay here. This is a brothel."

As if emphasizing Amy's declaration, a pair of footsteps, one heavy and the other light, mounted the staircase. A deep voice mixed with a high-pitched giggle filtered down the hall, and the door next to Amy's room opened and closed. Moments later, rhythmic banging commenced, causing Amy's eyes to widen and fresh tears to course down her cheeks.

"Will, I just can't," Amy said.

"I'll figure something out," Will said. "You need to stay here until I do, though. Can you give me a couple days?"

Amy nodded and sipped her caudle, which had cooled. She looked at Will, her eyes glistening. "I am a ruined woman."

"I will not listen to this, Amy. What happened has no bearing on your virtue," Will said, although he knew an unmarried woman who was no longer a virgin did have a stigma, even through no fault of her own.

Amy stayed in her small room all day, and Will remained with her for as long as he could. But when the shadows lengthened, he knew he had to return home before the gates at the bridge closed. After extracting a promise from Ellyn to watch over Amy, Will left, hurrying through the fading light. As he passed Culler's home, he considered bursting in and beating Culler to death. But Amy was right; then they both would be in dire straits. He vowed to exact his revenge, but not that night.

Will continued on, wrestling with his thoughts, his thin leather shoes growing wet from the snow that still lined the streets. As he turned down Fenn Road, he resolved to discuss Amy's situation with his parents. Perhaps she could move home until another, better posting could be found. Or maybe they could marry her to a kind man who would remove her from that lifestyle altogether.

THE FAILED APPRENTICE

Either way, Peter and Elizabeth would surely welcome their daughter home once they learned of Amy's brutal attack at the hands of her employer.

Yet when Will arrived home, Peter and Elizabeth were standing in front of the hearth, their voices raised. There was no sign of Will's siblings except for Kate, who, despite the shouting, slept soundly in her cradle. Both turned to Will as he entered the house.

"What?" Will said, looking from Peter to Elizabeth and back to Peter again.

"Hugh Culler was here this afternoon," Peter said. "Looking for Amy."

"Amy?" Will said, feigning ignorance.

"It seems your sister has run off, taking some of Culler's silver with her."

"I cannot believe that. Amy would not steal," Elizabeth shook her head. "We taught her better than that."

"Apparently, we didn't. She is spoiled, Elizabeth." Peter said, his voice escalating. "You have spoiled that girl! She could not handle domestic work. You did not teach her properly when she was young."

"You will not put this on me," Elizabeth said, crossing her arms.

"Theft is a hanging offense!" Peter said, ignoring his wife. "She could face the gibbet for this. And the shame she has brought on our family! Stupid girl."

Will saw how this would play out: Culler's word that his servant had fled with his silver would certainly discredit any accusations Amy might make.

"And he will be back!" Peter continued. "He won't let this rest. If I get hold of that girl before Culler, she'll wish she'd never been born."

Will quickly shelved any idea he had about broaching the subject of Amy's return. He would have to find another alternative. One that kept her safe and away from Culler and, clearly, their parents.

Chapter 8

The next morning Will left for the Axe just as the sun was coming up, closing the door softly, his tread light. Crossing the bridge, he eyed Culler's house. It was dark; no fine beeswax candles lit the mullioned windows. Again Will thought of bursting in, confronting Culler. He walked up to the door and tried the latch. If it was open, he would take that as a sign to enter and attack Culler. But the door was bolted. Will stood for a moment, his hand on the cold latch. He didn't have time for this. He needed to get to the Axe to check on Amy.

When Will arrived at the Axe, Amy was dressed and sitting in the front room. Her ruined servant's clothes had been replaced by a dress that Will recognized as Ivy's. Yet the low-cut bodice did little more than accentuate the darkening bruises above Amy's breasts, which enraged Will further. Nevertheless, Ellyn had done her best to clean Amy up. Her hair and face were washed, and a poultice had been applied to a deep gash on her arm. "You are looking better," Will said.

"Ellyn and the girls here have been kind."

Will sat on a heavy oak chair and relayed Culler's visit to the Pattens. "I was hoping you could go home, but, given their reaction to Culler, I'd avoid them." Will looked at his hands. "Perhaps our parents will soften over time."

Amy shook her head. "I am not your responsibility, Will. You have enough to deal with. I will go to the almshouse."

Will looked at her with disbelief. Almshouses were church-run institutions for the very poor. Although they provided housing and sometimes a small stipend, all the residents were indigent, and some ill or diseased. "You will not be going to the almshouse," Will said. "You said you would give me a couple days to devise a plan. And I will."

Although it was still early in the day, the door to the Axe opened, and two men walked in. Will moved his arm in front of

THE FAILED APPRENTICE

Amy to shield her, but he relaxed when he recognized the men Rich and Cobbe, who had become regular patrons. Ellyn rushed into the room from the back. "Master Rich, Master Cobbe, good morning to you," she said, curtseying.

"Ellyn," the man who Will assumed was Rich said. Rich looked at Amy, ignoring Will. "And who do we have here?"

Ellyn quickly moved between Amy and Rich. "Oh, she is not one of the girls," she said apologetically.

"A shame," Rich said. "She's a flower I'd like to pluck." Rich laughed at his joke and slapped Cobbe on the back.

Will rose from the chair and clenched his fists. "Will, I have some money for you to take to the bishop," Ellyn said, giving Will a steely glare.

Rich ignored Ellyn. "We'll have our regulars," he said. "And be quick about it. We are due in Westminster shortly." Then, leering at Amy, "Let me know if this one changes her mind. I'd like something to look forward to." Amy clenched her jaw and looked at the floor.

Once Rich and Cobbe were situated, Ellyn disappeared into the back and returned, holding a sack of coins. "I meant it about the money," she said, handing Will the heavy leather bag. "Take this to Nick. He's expecting you."

Will looked at Amy and back at Ellyn. "She'll be fine," Ellyn said. "I won't turn her into a whore while you're gone."

"Just keep her hidden in case Culler appears."

Amy stood and followed Ellyn into the back room; Will left the Axe, his eyes sweeping the street for Culler, who was nowhere to be seen.

Will arrived at Winchester Palace and stood under a large oak waiting for Nick. The wind howled off the Thames, wherries bouncing on the choppy waves, their passengers hunkered down to protect themselves from the cold.

Nick arrived shortly after Will. He pulled a pocket sundial from his cloak and opened it. "Just a bit past 10:00," he said, looking at the gilt box, a tight string pulled taut to capture the sun and cast a shadow on the roman numerals etched into the wood.

"That's quite nice," Will said, momentarily forgetting Amy. "May I see it?"

Nick handed Will the small sundial. "A present from Gardiner," he said proudly.

"It's a beauty," Will said, his finger tracing the numbers and small Tudor rose etched on the surface. Will reluctantly closed the sundial and handed it and his money sack to Nick.

Nick fastened the money sack to his belt and stumbled, pretending the weight of the pouch had upset his balance. "Things must be good at the Axe," he said, laughing.

"Ellyn is pulling in a lot of rich clients. Some are right chuffs."

Nick shrugged. "Not a surprise, but Gardiner will be happy," he said as he looked past the palace and away from the Stews. "I could do with some food. There's an alehouse close by I like. Come with me and have some mulled wine. That will warm us up."

At the mention of food, Will's stomach growled loudly. He had barely eaten yesterday and skirted out of the house too quickly that morning to even grab a heel of bread. Although he wanted to return to the Axe to keep an eye on Amy, Will felt himself following Nick down the street.

Because it was early, The Tabard Inn was empty, save a tired-looking serving girl, who regarded Will and Nick's entrance with a yawn. "Two mulled wines," Nick called to her, "and bring over a plate of cheese and bread."

Will and Nick sat at an old wooden table in the small, dark room, the cold winter sunlight seeping through the few windows. Nick took out his sundial and admired it again. "Gardiner's star is on the rise," he finally said. "King Henry likes him. The Bishopric of Winchester was a surprise for him. He did not expect such a prestigious appointment."

"You are lucky to be associated with him," Will said, then looked down at his hands, calloused from work, and began to poke at a splinter that had lodged in his thumb. The serving girl arrived with steaming mugs and a block of cheese and bread, precariously balanced on a thin wooden board.

THE FAILED APPRENTICE

"You seem distracted," Nick observed as he cut into the cheese.

Will sighed. He looked at Nick - here was a man close to his age, successfully aligned with a man on the political ascent. Will had begun to think of him as a friend but remained wary. Yet it would be good to unburden himself, to share his worries. "It's my sister," he began.

Will told Nick about Amy - from the spirited girl she had been, to taking a job with Culler, to her assault and subsequent hiding at the Axe. He felt his throat catch when he described how she had changed in the last several months - her thin hair, her pasty skin, her haunted eyes, her sadness and resignation. "I don't know what to do," he said.

Nick was silent for a moment. "I know Culler. He has a bad reputation. This news does not surprise me." He shook his head. "She could pursue this, swear out a complaint. But it's a long shot."

"She won't," Will said. "And Culler has accused her of stealing, so it would be her word against his. And we know who will be believed."

Nick nodded, tore a piece of bread from the load, and chewed. "I may have a solution," he finally said. "There could be a spot for her at the palace. It's a big place, and we could use another chambermaid. We just lost a girl. She ran off with one of the cooks."

For the first time in a while, Will felt himself relax. "That would be perfect," he said. "As long as it's a safe place for her. Culler can't know where she is, and she cannot handle another assault."

"The palace is safe; you can be sure of it. Bring her by this afternoon."

Will took a long drink of the mulled wine, which was cooling, but the scent of cloves and cinnamon was still strong and lingered in the air. It was a good solution, this work at Winchester Palace. He could hardly wait to tell Amy.

That afternoon Will and Amy walked the short distance to the palace, Will constantly scanning the street for Culler. Nick met them outside the heavy, wooden doors. "You must be Amy," Nick said, bowing low. Amy blushed in return. "Let's go inside. I'll introduce you to the housekeeper and get you situated."

Will and Amy stopped and stared once they entered Winchester Palace's great hall. Never had they seen anything so magnificent. The ceiling soared forty-two feet above them and ended in an intricate crisscross of dark wood beams. Believed to be constructed under the guidance of master craftsman Henry Yevele, the hall spread out in front of them - lengthy, wide, and opulent, with smaller rooms nestled to the side. Intricate frescoes lined the walls, biblical allegories and pastoral scenes surrounded by serpentine vines and flowers. Light cascaded from the imposing rose window at the opposite end of the hall, warming the tightly woven rush mats that lined the floor. "Close your mouth, Will," Nick said. "You are gaping."

"It's hard not to. My family's house could fit in here ten times over!"

"You get used to it," Nick said, laughing. "Come." He led Will and Amy through the hall, their treads softened on the rush mats. At the end of the hall, he turned and entered one of the side rooms. "Mistress Clark," Nick said. An older woman jumped and turned to Nick, her hand clutching her chest.

"For the love of all that's holy, you scared the devil out of me, Master Greene," she said, gasping for air and bowing her head slightly, her Scottish brogue thick. Regaining her composure, she looked at Will and Amy. "This must be the lass you were telling me about."

Will gave Amy a little shove. She stepped forward and curtseyed. "This is Amy," Nick said. "She has prior experience as a domestic, as I told you."

Mistress Clark nodded knowingly. "So, your master was a grabber?"

"Worse," Will added. Amy looked down, twisting the fabric of her skirt into a ball.

"Well, there be none of that here. You can be assured of that. We keep a tight household. No funny business." Mistress Clark

THE FAILED APPRENTICE

smiled. Will noticed that the only teeth she appeared to have were three in the front.

Amy continued to stare at the floor, her eyes glazing over.

"Come here, my lass," Mistress Clark said. "You be all right here. You'll be safe."

Amy took a tentative step forward, and Mistress Clark took her hand.

"Let's go," Nick said to Will. "Mistress Clark has everything under control. Amy will be fine."

Amy looked at Will, panic rising on her face. "Thank you both," she said, her voice breaking. Will could see she was scared, that this new post was as much frightening as it was a relief. "Everything will work out, Amy. Remember, I am just down the street," he said.

"Enough!" Mistress Clark said. "She is a hearty lass and will do just fine here. No blubbering! Now be gone. I best get Amy in proper clothes and explain her duties."

Will nodded, and he and Nick turned to leave. "She will be safe here?" Will whispered to Nick as they crossed the great hall.

"She will," Nick said. "I will keep an eye out. Do not worry."

Chapter 9

Will was able to relax during the next few weeks. Amy was safely ensconced at the palace, and Will's earnings from the Axe were growing. One winter evening, Will left the Axe with two shillings from Ellyn jingling in his small leather pouch. Although cold, there was no wind as Will crossed the bridge and took the circuitous route home.

Yet when Will opened the door, he saw something was amiss. As usual, his brothers were rolling around on the floor, but his parents were standing beside the trestle table, scowling. Will looked at his mother, who looked exhausted and much older than her forty years. Then he saw the bag in the center of the table - his money bag, the bag which had been hidden under his pallet for the last three months.

Peter looked at Will, picked up the bag, and dropped it heavily on the table. Will's brothers stopped wrestling and looked up, the thud registering on their faces. Will said nothing.

"Well?" Peter said.

"Well, what?" Will replied, his throat suddenly dry.

"We found this sack, full of coins, hidden under your pallet!"

Will tried to think fast, but his mind felt as if it was moving through molasses. "It's my savings," he stammered.

By now, Will's brothers sat, eyes wide, staring at the drama unfolding around them.

"Savings!" Peter's voice boomed. "You have hoarded almost ten pounds, hidden under your bed, yet our family starves!"

"No one is starving," Will said. "I have given you money as I have earned it. And as I recall, we have had meat on our table and fire in the hearth since I have returned home!"

"Will," Elizabeth began, her hand touching her husband's arm, her voice steady but with a worried edge. "Please explain."

"Yes, do that," Peter said, twisting his arm roughly away from Elizabeth's grip. "You are clearly not working for a blacksmith, as I have long suspected."

THE FAILED APPRENTICE

Will's mind whirled. He had kept so much from his family - his job, Amy - he did not know where to begin.

"Well? Surely this question is not a difficult one," Peter spat, his eyes blazing.

"I am working at the Axe, doing repairs," Will finally said. "It's all I could get after the Blacksmith Guild rejected me."

"The Sharpened Axe?" Peter said, his face reddening. "That bawdy house in Southwark?"

"What's a "bawdy house?"" Will's brother John piped in.

"That vipers' nest?" Elizabeth said, ignoring John. "Will, how could you? This is beyond shameful."

"This is ill-begotten money, coins from sinful men, tainted money," Peter shouted. "How dare you bring it into this house?"

Will had had enough. He stood up straighter, his eyes meeting Peter's. "This money fed you, clothed you, and kept the house warm," he said. "You didn't care where it came from as long as it met your purposes."

Peter picked up the money sack and hurled it across the room at Will. The bag was secured with a strong leather string, yet the force of impact on Will's chest caused a few pence to fall out and land on the floor.

"Money!" John said as he grabbed a coin.

"It's bad enough that we have Culler sniffing around here, now this," Peter said. "Get out and take your coins with you. I hope they serve you well. You are a liar and an immoral man, Will. You have dishonored this family. You are no longer welcome in our home."

"Dishonored?" Will said as he picked up the money sack from the floor, a reed stuck to its side. He pulled the drawstring tight. "By doing honest labor?"

"Working at a stew house is not honest labor, regardless of the capacity of the job."

Will looked at his mother. Surely she would not go along with this. But Elizabeth pursed her lips, shook her head, and turned her back on Will. "Very well," Will said. "I will go. And you will miss my coins."

Will narrowed his eyes at his father, giving him a beat to change his mind, to apologize. Instead, Peter snarled, "Enjoy spending your sullied money."

Will turned and left the house. The door, which had always been loose and cracked, was newly repaired. Probably with my money, Will thought, as he slammed it shut.

Fenn Road was dark as Will left the house, and candles blazed in windows along the street. At Fenn Road's end, he turned and headed toward Southwark. Although London Bridge's gates were certainly closed by now, he hoped to get near enough to Southwark to be able to pass into it at first light. A few tenements near Winchester Palace had rooms for let; Will was sure he could secure lodging from one in the morning. Although they were often dirty and crowded, it would be a convenient place to stay until he got his bearings, and his money could keep him out of the worst of them. He'd find a room close to the Axe and close to Amy. It was a good plan.

Moving through the darkness, Will was all too aware of his bulging coin pouch hidden under his cloak. He scanned the street for an inn where he could spend the night, get off the streets, and hole up in a room. The Hoop, a tavern dating back to the 14th century, loomed ahead; he had been there before, and it was a welcoming spot with decent food and small bedchambers above the main room. With luck, the Hoop would have a room he could use for the night. He would sort out his now uncertain housing situation in the morning.

The Hoop was filling up with people when Will arrived. He spotted the innkeeper, a tall, fat man standing next to a large trestle table, directing serving girls who carried tankards of ale or bowls of pottage. "Could I have a room for the night?" Will asked.

"A room for a single man?" the innkeeper asked, lounging against a post as he eyed Will.

"Yes," Will replied.

"A shared room? Or one just for yourself?"

"Just for me."

"Just a room?" The innkeeper winked at Will.

THE FAILED APPRENTICE

"Just a room."

"All right then. Upstairs, third door on the right. That will be a shilling. We provide a basin with fresh water, too."

Will opened his coin pouch and removed the shilling. The innkeeper's eyes widened at the size of the bag. "Surely you be wanting something to drink, sir?" the innkeeper said, smiling, standing up a bit straighter. "We have some fine ales and some hearty stews." He patted his stomach, which jiggled in response.

Will looked around him. A fire burned high in the hearth, and men were sitting at long tables drinking and eating, clearly enjoying themselves. Will knew he should go upstairs and hunker down with his money. But he was hungry, thirsty, and anger toward his family simmered dangerously close to the surface. "I will have some ale," Will said. "And a meat stew."

Will sat at the end of a long table beside a man slurping pottage out of a wooden bowl. The thin broth dribbled down his chin and pooled on his heavy wool tunic. He turned to Will and smiled. "Good food," he said, licking his lips.

Moments later, a serving girl placed a tankard of ale and a bowl of beef stew in front of Will. "Oh, you be getting the meat!" Will's neighbor commented, eyeing the contents of Will's bowl. "You must be rich."

"I'm not rich, just hungry," Will said, hoisting the tankard to his lips and drinking. The beer was fresh and Will drained the mug in no time. He motioned to the serving girl and pointed to the tankard. She nodded and disappeared into the crowd.

The stew was also surprisingly good. It was hot and well-seasoned, although somewhat skimpy on the meat. Will quickly finished his meal and second ale and felt himself relax.

By now, a small crowd was filling the tavern. Will was warm, sated, and more relaxed than he had been in weeks. The man next to him smiled and burped. "Another ale?" he asked. "If you get one, then I will too."

Another drink sounded great to Will. His new friend was grimy but seemed friendly enough. It would be pleasant to pass the time with someone who didn't speak of whores, heretics, or ways in which Will was a disappointment.

Two more ales appeared on the table, and Will took a long draw on his. "My name's Fergus," the man said. "Named after me old man."

"I'm Will, named after no one," Will replied, his voice slurring slightly.

The man finished his ale in one long swig. "I got some dice," he said. "Fancy a game of chance? A little wager?"

Nick had played dice with Amy and his brothers; he was lucky at games of chance. "I'll give it a go," he said. "But just a small wager. Just a pence or two."

"Hazard?" The man asked.

Hazard was a well-known dice game with fluid rules, none of which Will understood. Will shook his head. "I'm not sure how to play."

"Then how about a game of nine five?"

Will smiled. Nine five, or novem cinque, was an easy game. Each player rolled two dice; the first to get either a five or nine lost. "We'll start with a pence," the man said, reaching into his bag and extracting a small coin. He placed it on the table and Will did the same. Then Fergus produced two sets of dice and handed Will one. Will looked at the square made of bone. The dots were faded and worn. Clearly, these dice had seen some action.

By the luck of the roll, Will began. Roll after roll, he managed to avoid five or nine, while Fergus was not so lucky. Finally, after ten wins, Will's roll ended up showing nine. "Ten wins!" Fergus said, "That's a good run. Now maybe I can win some of my coins back." Will looked over, surprised to see his tankard had been refilled.

But Will's new friend's luck did not change. Although he won one game, Will won three more, and the bet increased to several pence. Will won two more games and wondered how this new friend could allow himself to lose so much money.

THE FAILED APPRENTICE

After Will won the next game, Fergus stood up. "Going out to piss," he said. "And pray to the gods for some luck." Will watched as Fergus stumbled to the door.

Will motioned for another ale. As he waited for Fergus, he thought about his family - how Peter struggled, a victim of his own making. Will chuckled to himself. Making money wasn't so hard. His work at the Axe wasn't easy, but it wasn't too difficult, either. And he had won over a shilling just by throwing some dice.

Moments later, Fergus staggered back to the table, knocked into it, and sent both tankards and dice flying. As he bent down to pick up the mess, he murmured loud enough for Will to hear, "guess I've had a bit too much ale!"

Will, too, was feeling the effects of drink. But he was warm, happy, and confident. The barmaid brought over fresh tankards, and Fergus handed Will's dice back to him. "Perhaps my luck will change," he slurred. "Couldn't get much worse."

And change it did. After Fergus' sojourn outside, he won the next game and the next. Will quickly saw his winnings dwindle, then disappear. "How about we increase our wager?" Fergus said. Will agreed. He was lucky. He was sure to win back his losses and more.

But after an hour of mostly losses, Will's money sack contained just a shilling and three pence. His head swam from ale and the cloying heat of the tavern, and his stomach roiled. Fergus' face swam in and out of Will's vision. Just how much ale had he consumed?

"I believe you've had enough," Fergus snorted as Will's head slumped onto the table. He took the dice from Will's hand and pocketed them. "Pleasure doing business with you."

From his vantage point of the tabletop, Will watched as Fergus stood, pushed in his chair, and walked across the tavern to the door - not a lurch or stumble to his gait. Will closed his eyes and felt the room spin. If he could just stand and get to his room, he could sleep off the drink and protect the few coins he had left. But moving his legs seemed impossible, and his head felt like lead. He'd just rest for a moment.

Will awoke to the innkeeper kicking his chair. "Wake up, you sod," he said. "Go to your room. Thank God you paid me before that prigman cozened you."

Will looked up, confused. The tavern was dark; it must be late. He felt his cloak for his money bag, only to discover it was gone. He looked around but knew it was useless. He had lost everything he had saved, including his leather sack. Will's stomach rolled over, and he vomited on the floor.

THE FAILED APPRENTICE

Chapter 10

Will left the Hoop as day was breaking. His head pounded, and he squinted against the sun cresting over the Thames. The winter morning was cold, with ice glistening off the cobbled streets, but Will barely noticed. His thoughts were consumed with worries over more pressing matters - where he would sleep and how he could afford to eat.

Will arrived at the Axe, and all seemed quiet. At the sound of the door closing, Ellyn emerged from the back, took one look at Will, and laughed. "You seem worse for wear. A bit too much of the drink last night?"

Will's clothes were creased and dirty, and a thin residue of vomit lined his cloak. He knew he must smell as bad as he looked. His eyes stung, his head throbbed, and, for a moment, his throat tightened as he held back tears. He collapsed onto one of the chairs by the fire and cradled his head in his hands. "I don't know what to do," he said, barely audible but loud enough for Ellyn to hear.

Will told Ellyn everything that occurred - from his father's rejection to being swindled out of what was, to Will, a small fortune. "I have no place to live and no money to survive," he said, his eyes finally meeting Ellyn's.

Ellyn knelt until her face was level with Will's. Although her breath reeked from her rotting teeth, her eyes were kind. "You cannot stay here," she said. "As much as I would like it. It is a stew house and no place for a man to live. But I do know someone who lives on Bear Lane. He has a small room where you could stay until you have enough money for a proper place. He owes me a favor."

Will nodded and felt the tension start to release from his shoulders. "That is very generous," he said.

"Don't thank me until you've seen it. It's no palace." Ellyn hoisted herself to a standing position. "Now go wash the puke off your clothes. Once you're presentable, I'll send you over to him."

The room on Bear Lane was barely larger than Will's room on Fenn Road but dirtier, darker, and smellier. The proprietor, Andrew Cole, was a short, thin man with a face that resembled a ferret, up to and including tiny, beady black eyes. "You can stay here for a week for four pence," he said. "That price is a favor to Ellyn. Then the price goes up to a pence a day."

Even in the straits Will found himself in, he understood that a pence a day for what amounted to a trash receptacle was robbery. But he was in no position to argue. "Very well," he said, surveying the pallet on the floor, covered in stains and barely thicker than a slice of bread.

Will spent a sleepless night on Bear Lane. The scrabbling of rats on the floors, the stench rising from his pallet, and the yells of drunkards outside the tenement proved exhausting. He slunk back to the Axe the next morning, tired and demoralized. Thankfully, Ellyn provided him with fresh water to clean away the night's sweat and grime.

When Will appeared in the front room after washing his face, he noticed a book lying on a low table. "What's this?" he asked Ellyn as he picked up the leather volume and read the title.

"It's a book, obviously," Ellyn said. "Some high and mighty sop left it yesterday. He'll be back for it, you can be sure. Books be valuable."

Will sat down and opened the book. It was *Aesop's Fables*, translated into English by William Caxton. The book's leather binding was worn but of high quality; the pages were marked by annotations. Although the book's images looked woodcut and rudimentary, the text was clear and easy to read. Will began to read the fable of the wolf and crane.

Ellyn opened her mouth to chastise Will, who should not be reading but working, when the door opened and regulars Rich and Cobbe entered. "Gentlemen," she said, smiling.

THE FAILED APPRENTICE

As usual, Rich spoke first. "Our regulars, Ellyn," he said. "And make haste." As Ellyn scurried into the back to find the girls, Rich approached Will. "What's that?" he said.

Will stood up, unnerved. "A book of fables," he said. "It was left by someone yesterday. Ellyn is sure he'll be back for it. It's a fine book."

Rich looked at him quizzically. "You can read?"

Will nodded and smiled, oddly proud of not only his ability to read but surprising Rich with it.

Ellyn returned to the room with Avis and Ivy in tow, who curtsied to their clients. Rich handed Ellyn a few coins. "This should cover it," he said and turned to Will. "Take this," Rich said, removing his heavy wool cloak and throwing it at Will. "Put it by the fire; it's wet from the snow." He turned and marched up the stairs, followed by Cobbe and the girls.

Ellyn turned to Will, who was draping Rich's cloak over a chair near the fire. "This room needs cleaning. You need to remove these dirty rushes," she said, gesturing to the loose reeds on the floor. "I've invested in mats."

Aside from prostitution, bear baiting, and cock fighting, Southwark was known for manufacturing rush mats. They were pricier than the loose reeds most places still used as floor covering. However, as Ellyn attempted to raise the standards of the Axe, it was fitting she would splurge for mats. "And when you're done," she continued, "I have lavender boughs that need breaking up. Scatter those on the floor as well. We want the place to smell nice."

Will began the dirty work of gathering the old rushes together and carting them outside. They had not been changed in several weeks, and mouse turds and rotting food were caught in the rough reeds, which scratched his hands. Will's head pounded, and his back ached. After only fifteen minutes of work, his head began to swim. He sat down and massaged his temples.

Will regarded his surroundings. He had hauled most of the rushes out of the room, and a thin haze of dust and reed detritus swirled in the air. He coughed and cursed Fergus for stealing his money. He had been a fool.

The fire was crackling, and Will noticed Rich's cloak was sending up plumes of steam. Not good, Will thought. He'll be furious if his cloak is too hot or worse, burned when he returns. Will stood and gathered the cloak, intent on moving it further from the fire. Yet as he held the heavy, expensive garment, he felt the familiar weight of a money bag attached to the lining. Will felt for the sack; it was big, heavy, and obviously contained a significant number of coins. Will remembered Culler and the ease of that theft. Surely a man as wealthy as Richard Rich would not miss a couple shillings. And besides, Rich was not a nice man. He was rude to Ellyn and Ivy. He treated Will as a servant, or worse. And he had looked lustfully at Amy. A small theft was justifiable. And would, most likely, go unnoticed.

Will turned the cloak so the lining and money bag were exposed and ran his hands down the fur lining. A man this wealthy, he would not need or miss a few coins. Will sat with the cloak on his lap and untied the leather money bag. He was correct; the bag was filled with gold and silver.

Yet just as Will reached in and felt the cold, smooth coins, footsteps sounded overhead. Rich began descending the stairs laughing with Cobbe but stopped when he saw Will.

"Well, well. I see we have a little thief," he said, walking down the stairs and crossing the room.

At this, Ellyn entered the room. It took her no more than a moment to assess the situation. "Will," she said, panic crossing her face. "What are you thinking?"

"He's thinking he's going to make off with my coins," Rich said, grabbing Will and hauling him to his feet.

"I wasn't," Will stammered. "I was just moving your cloak away from the fire."

"I didn't realize you needed to have your hand in my money sack to move my cloak," Rich said, tightening his grip on Will.

THE FAILED APPRENTICE

Rich pulled Will out the door and onto the street. "Constable!" he yelled, searching the road. A few passersby stopped and stared. "Constable!" Rich called again, louder.

Ellyn shot out behind Rich and Will. "Master Rich, please," she said. "I'm sure there's an explanation for all this. Will is a good lad."

"He is neither good nor a lad," Rich said, still scanning the street for a constable.

Will attempted to wrench his forearm from Rich's grip. "You best not struggle, or you'll be in a worse situation than you currently are," Rich seethed.

Moments later, a constable turned the corner. Rich began waving his free hand over his head. "Constable! Over here."

The constable, a young man with a pale face and bulging eyes, inched over to Rich, looking panic-stricken. Like most constables in London, this one was from the lower echelon of society and a resident of the district where he served. Many men appointed to the office refused to accept the appointment, often preferring to pay a fine than take on the responsibilities entrusted to the position. As a result, constables such as the one creeping toward Rich were more the rule than the exception.

"Take this thief into custody," Rich said, releasing his grip on Will's arm and roughly pushing him toward the officer. "I found him rifling through my money sack."

The constable took ahold of Will but looked confused. "What do you want me to do with him?" he asked.

"By God's nails," Rich said, taking off his cap and hitting the constable with it. "How should I know? Take him to the Tower. That's as good a place as any."

The constable looked horrified. "The Tower *of London*?" he asked.

Rich rolled his eyes. "Yes, you idiot. The Tower of London."

The constable looked at Will almost apologetically. "Come on, then," he said, pulling Will away from Rich and Ellyn. "To the Tower you go."

Will and the constable slogged through the cold mid-morning air to the Tower. "What's going to happen to me?" Will asked as they crossed the bridge.

"I don't know," the constable replied apathetically. "You may be branded. You may be killed. Or your hand may be chopped off."

Will felt his head grow hot, his eyes start to swim, his ears begin to ring. He lost his balance and tripped. "Up you go," the constable said, hoisting Will to his feet and continuing to the Tower.

Will was placed in a small cell below ground in the Tower, so deep that no light entered the room. The packed dirt floors were littered with corpses of vermin and rags from earlier prisoners, surrounding Will with a miasma of urine, vomit, and decay. The room barely afforded enough space for Will to stand and take a few paces. He sat, crouched, with his back against the cold stone walls, willing his eyes to adjust to the blackness. How did he get to this point? He blamed Topside, Fergus, his father, Rich. Will buried his head in his hands and cried.

Time proved intangible in Will's cramped cell. The howls of other prisoners, the heavy steps of guards, and the scrabbling of rats seemed to herald the passage of minutes or hours. Because of the lack of light, Will had no idea if day had transitioned into night. At one point, a jailer wrenched Will's door open and shoved in a bowl of thin gruel. "Wait," Will yelled. "What's happening to me?" His entreaties were ignored as the door slammed shut, the hard metal bolt sliding into place, causing Will's heart to sink. He thought of Nick's pocket sundial. Even a piece as fine as that would have no use here, where darkness was perpetual.

Will pushed the gruel into the far corner of his little cell. Perhaps that will keep the rats away from him, he thought as he huddled in the corner, shaking. He closed his eyes and prayed for sleep or death. He would welcome any form of oblivion to get him out of this hellhole, even for a few minutes.

THE FAILED APPRENTICE

Will managed to doze a bit, waking with a start as his head bobbed forward. He was aware of the movement of rats and bugs, crawling and scampering about the floor, sometimes skittering over Will's feet, which he tried to pull in as close to his body as possible. The rats had found their way to his bowl of what he thought was his supper. He could hear them fighting for the food he refused to eat.

Will remained balled up against the stone wall until his muscles cramped. As he tried to extend his legs, fighting against the pain, he heard voices outside his cell and the rough grinding of the bolt as the door creaked open. Two guards stood outside, one holding a lantern, the light casting long shadows into the cell, which were swallowed up in the darkness. "Get up," the one without the lantern said. "You have a visitor upstairs."

Will staggered to his feet, his legs screaming in pain. The guard grabbed his arm and dragged him through the blackened corridors and up narrow, winding stone steps. "Who is here for me?" he asked.

"Shut up," the guard holding the lantern replied.

Will was dragged up four flights of stairs, each one a bit brighter, a bit cleaner, than the previous. At the final landing, Will was pushed toward a large door that opened to a room with large windows from which daylight streamed in. Richard Rich sat at the head of a long table, a goblet in front of him, a smirk on his face.

Chapter 11

Will was propelled into the room, and the door closed loudly and abruptly behind him. "Sit," Rich said.

Will slowly walked to the table, his legs still wobbly from his night in the cell. He pulled out the nearest chair and sat, placing his hands on the table. It was a fine table, dark wood, perhaps mahogany. The sides of it were engraved with Tudor roses.

"You are filthy, and I can smell you from here," Rich said, waving his hand in front of his face.

"I've been in a dungeon," Will said. "No one has paid mind to my comforts."

Rich took a sip from his jeweled goblet, the gems glistening in the light. "Do you know who I am?" he asked.

"You are Master Rich."

"But do you know *who I am*?"

"I know you are a man of some importance," Will said. "But that's all I know."

Rich leaned back, his blond hair resting on the chair's ornate wood backing. "*Some* importance, I guess you could say that," he said, laughing. "I am about to be appointed Attorney General for Wales. I am a Member of Parliament. I have the king's ear. I guess you could say I am a man of *some* importance."

Will nodded, surprised at Rich's credentials. To him, he was just a pompous gent who liked Ellyn's whores. Rich continued to stare at him. Finally, Will lowered his head and said, "my lord."

Rich leaned across the table and shoved a piece of paper at Will. "Here," Rich said. "Read this. Aloud."

Will looked at the paper - a thin parchment with black letters swimming on it. His eyes stung from lack of sleep, the strain of trying to see in the inky darkness of the dungeon, and the brightness of the room where he currently found himself. He had trouble focusing. He cleared his throat and began reading, his

THE FAILED APPRENTICE

voice hoarse. "My name is Parrot, a bird of Paradise, by nature devised of a wondrous kind," he began.

"Enough," Rich said, snatching the paper back. "You read this trifling poem easily. You are obviously educated."

"Yes," Will stammered.

"I needed to be sure you weren't using that book at the Axe as a prop."

Will shook his head. Rich pulled back from the table. "Do you know the penalties for stealing, especially from a man as influential as I am? Losing your hand would be the best outcome for you. More likely, you will hang."

Will gulped.

"However, I am offering you a way out. A way where we both get what we want. You get to live. I get," Rich hesitated. "Information."

Will looked at Rich. He was not a large man, but his presence filled the room. There was not a drop of insecurity about his demeanor. Nor mercy.

"It is unusual to find an educated man, such as yourself, in such a predicament," Rich waved his hand in Will's direction, a large ruby ring sending sprays of light onto the table, "Stealing and working in a brothel - a most unusual career choice indeed. Your morals are clearly fluid. I like that in a man."

Will sat up straighter. He was not a man lacking in morals. A flame of resentment began to burn in his stomach. "I've done what is necessary to survive," he said. "That is all."

Rich gave a little snort. "You want to live; that's obvious. So I take it my proposal may be something you'd be interested in? Work for me or face the rope?"

"I am interested," Will said with no hesitation. If whatever Rich proposed was what was needed to remain alive, he would do it, no matter what was involved.

"Of course you are." Rich leaned forward, his long fingers tenting in front of his thin lips. His eyes squinted, and he breathed deeply. Then he sat back. "Just know, I can have you killed in a blink of an eye. You'll be hanging from the gallows before you knew what hit you. So if there's even a whiff of deceit on your part...."

"No, my lord. No deceit," Will said. "I value my life."

"Very well. Let's start off simply. We have come to suspect that there are merchants in London who have become involved with smuggling. Greedy men lining their pockets at the expense of the Crown. Such behavior is stealing, and I have no tolerance for theft," Rich looked pointedly at Will. "I will place you in the Mercers' Hall. You will keep your ears open and report everything you hear directly to me, whether you deem it relevant or not."

"I have no training in being a merchant," Will said, a bead of sweat trickling down his back.

"You won't *be* a merchant," Rich said, rolling his steely blue eyes. "I'll have you installed as a courier. You will do as instructed; keep your mouth shut and your ears open. If you're successful, you will keep yourself alive."

Will nodded. Tired, hungry, dirty, and desperate, he would have agreed to anything.

"Very good," Rich said. He clapped his hands and a burly servant appeared, the scar bisecting his cheek alluding to work that transcended mere servitude. The man hoisted Will up by the arm, so much so that Will's feet barely touched the floor. "Angus, take him to Islington," Rich commanded, pointing at Will. "And get him cleaned up. He's disgusting."

Rich's house in Islington abutted Newington Green, King Henry's park. The large, luxurious moated manor was a far cry from the filth of the Tower dungeon. Soaring ceilings, walls lined with jewel-toned tapestries, mullioned windows, and delicately woven rugs all attested to Rich's position of power and wealth. It was a different world from Southwark.

Will did not have much time to gawk, though. He was promptly bathed, dressed in new clothes, and ushered into a large chamber that overlooked the park. A canopied bed, curtained in red velvet and edged in fur, took up most of the room. The mattress was deep and, no doubt, filled with feathers, a far cry from the razor-thin

THE FAILED APPRENTICE

pallets on which Will had been sleeping. "Stay here if you know what's good for you. Don't go wandering off or try to escape," Angus sneered. "The cook will send food up."

While Will waited for food, he looked out the window next to the bed. The leaded glass, encased in a wrought-iron frame, distorted Will's view, but only slightly. He could see the park and several deer grazing, foraging through the frosty grass, the dappled light scattered across their brown and white coats. If he craned his neck, he could see homes on either side, both large, moated, and made of brick and timber. Behind the house to his right, he saw a garden, the stalks of dead flowers bent in the winter cold.

Will sat on the bed and felt himself sink into the mattress. The coverlet was soft, and Will lay down, just for a moment, he thought. Just to rest his eyes. He was asleep before this thought was fully formed.

The room was dark when Will awoke, the only light coming from a beeswax candle burning on a bedside table. Next to the candle sat a steaming bowl of stew and a tankard of beer. Will sat up, rubbed his eyes, and grabbed the spoon next to the stew. He ate so quickly that he barely had time to process the spices blended with the meat and vegetables. They were deep, rich, heady. Very different from his mother's thin pottage.

In minutes the stew bowl and tankard were empty. Will blew out the candle, climbed under the coverlet, and was asleep as his head hit the pillow.

Angus stormed into Will's room the next morning, pulled the coverlet from Will's sleeping body, and yelled, "Get your skinny arse up. The master wants to see you." He grimaced at Will and left the room.

Will climbed out of bed and stretched, although his heart hammered at the thought of seeing Rich. He splashed his face with water from a nearby basin and drew his fingers through his hair. He had slept in his clothes and was far from presentable, but what did Rich expect?

Will opened the door from his chamber and peered into the empty, darkened hall. A wide staircase lay before him, the banister a dark, highly polished wood. Creeping out of his room and down the stairs, Will listened for clues to where he could find Rich but was distracted by the grandeur of the home. Every surface gleaned, every wall was covered in ornate tapestries.

Angus appeared from around the corner. "In here," he barked before disappearing again.

Will followed Angus into a large hall, a vast stone fireplace abutting the paneled wall, large logs crackling and spewing sparks up the chimney. Rich looked up from a polished table as Will entered but said nothing, his mouth full of food. Rich waved his hand at a chair near the door. Will sat. Rich swallowed. "And so it begins," Rich finally said, a cold smile settling on his face.

THE FAILED APPRENTICE

Chapter 12

The following day, Rich and Will took a carriage to the Mercers' Hall in Cheapside. The Worshipful Company of Mercers was a large guild representing London merchants, principally ones importing and exporting wool and fine fabrics, but also those who focused on oils, spices, and other luxury goods. Established by charter in 1394, the order was thought to predate that date by centuries.

Rich spent the previous day with Will telling him what to look and listen for while at the guild. He groomed him on to how to act and terms with which he should be acquainted. "Remember what we went over yesterday," Rich said as the carriage bumped along the cobbled streets. "Also, you will be going by Will Jones. Jones is a common enough name to keep suspicion at bay. Apparently, your father is a respected draper." Rich scoffed and rolled his eyes. "We can't have anyone making the connection."

"Will Jones," Will said, trying out his new name.

"And you will check in with me at least once a week. When you find something incriminating, I need to know immediately."

"I understand," Will said.

"And I have arranged for you to live in a room on Bow Lane. Here is the address." Rich handed Will a crumpled piece of paper on which an address was scrawled. "It's not much, but it's better than the Tower."

When the carriage pulled up to the Mercers' Hall, Rich threw the door open and leapt out. "Come on, Master Jones," he said. "You have a job to do."

The Mercers' Hall shared an entrance with the Church of St. Thomas of Acon, the birthplace of St. Thomas Becket, the massive stone facade towering over the street teeming with merchants and shoppers. Rich strode purposefully into the hall, passing under the sculpture of a woman's head, her hair spread out and covering her shoulders, the motto of the mercers, *Honor*

Deo, engraved beneath. Will struggled to keep up with Rich, keep his nerves in check, and act like he knew what he was doing. Yet the sheer grandeur of the hall overwhelmed him. Ornate tapestries and banners hung from the walls, and stone tiling and heavy rugs covered the floor. The air was full with conversation and laughter. Yet when Rich entered the hall, all activity ceased, and all eyes turned to stare. Will was impressed. How could this slight man command such a response from the wealthiest merchants of London?

It was not long before an opulently dressed man approached Will and Rich. "Richard," he said. "What a surprise to see you at our humble hall."

Rich laughed. "Humble, my arse," he said. "You mercers are making coin hand over fist. This hall is even larger than my place in Islington. And almost as nicely decorated."

The man shrugged his shoulders. "I admit business is not bad," he said. "There's always a market for high-quality goods."

Rich nodded and smiled. Then, motioning to Will, he proceeded. "Owen, let me introduce you to Will Jones. Will's uncle is a mercer in Bristol. He hopes to bring Will into the business, but Will needs some training first. I hope you can use him for a bit. Perhaps as a courier? It's free labor. It would be a favor to both Will's father and me."

"Yes, yes, we can always use a courier," the man stammered. He turned to Will. "I'm Owen Dauntesey, Master of the Guild."

Will bowed his head. "Master Dauntesey, I am at your service."

Rich and Dauntesey engaged in small talk for a moment, then Rich turned to leave. He leaned in close to Will. "Smuggling is rampant in Bristol," he whispered. "Imply you are aware of how this side business works. Keep your ears open. I expect a full report. Otherwise," Rich raked a finger across his neck and grinned at Will. Then he was gone.

Will looked around him. Activity resumed at almost a feverish pitch the moment Rich left the hall. Will looked expectantly at Dauntesey. "Where do I begin?" he asked.

THE FAILED APPRENTICE

Owen Dauntesey sighed. "Rich seems to think it's acceptable to deposit young men on my doorstep and expect me to train them," he said, his lips pursing. "Very well. It appears neither of us has a choice in the matter. You say you will work as a courier?"

Will nodded. "I will do whatever is required of me."

"I have some documents you can take to Gray's Inn. Do you know where that is?"

Although Will knew Gray's Inn was one of the Inns of Court, he had no idea where it was. But he would never admit that. "I do," he said.

"Very well. Let me get them." Dauntesey disappeared into the hall and was immediately swallowed up by men asking him questions or engaging him in conversation. Fifteen minutes later, he returned with two scrolls of paper tied with heavy twine. "Hand these to the clerk at Gray's," he said. "Come back when you're done. They may have something for me."

Will took the scrolls and headed out the door onto Cheapside. "Cheap" was the medieval term for "markets," and Cheapside was teeming with them even on such a cold winter's day. Roads leading into the main thoroughfare were named after the products which could be purchased there: Ironmongers Lane, Bread Street, Poultry Street, Milk Street. Will recalled Nick telling him Thomas More was raised on Milk Street. Will briefly glanced down the narrow road. He wondered in which house More had lived and what forces made him into the man he was today.

Will approached Cheapside Cross, a tall monument in honor of Eleanor of Aquitaine, the wife of King Edward I. Restored in the 15th century and regilded once a decade, the gold was wearing thin in places but, nevertheless, remained a sight to behold. Will approached a well-dressed man who was lingering by the cross. "Excuse me," he said. "Can you tell me how to get to Gray's Inn?"

The man laughed and pointed down the road. "It's in Holborn, about a mile from here," he said. "You have a hike."

Will sighed. He knew where Holborn was; it was indeed a hike.

Will walked on, and when the streets became less crowded, he slipped down an alley and untied the documents. If they contained evidence of smuggling, then this would be an easy job. Furtively, he unrolled each scroll but was disappointed that they were simply a list of wool vendors in London. Nothing incriminating there.

Will arrived at Gray's Inn close to mid-morning. He was offered a hot roll by the clerk, who thanked him for the scrolls and tipped him two pence. He handed Will a scroll which he didn't bother to secure with twine and sent Will on the mile journey back. Based upon the relaxed demeanor of the clerk, this untied scroll was of little importance.

The day ended with Will no closer to uncovering smuggling or other nefarious deeds than when it began. Although it was only the first day, Will had been hopeful that he could quickly do what Rich expected and then move on with his life. But it seemed as though this was not how it was going to unfold.

Will left the Mercers' Hall and found Bow Lane easily. It was just off Cheapside and a short walk. Towering at the end of the street was St. Mary-le-Bow, an ancient church whose bells were melodic, although deafening, and rang throughout the day and again at 9:00 pm, marking London's curfew. The church had gone through many incarnations from its origin as a Norman church in 1080. A violent tornado destroyed the church in 1091. It was rebuilt but destroyed again in a fire in 1196. The original Norman undercroft crypt still existed, but the church itself had been rebuilt and cast a tall shadow over the narrow street.

Will found the address he was looking for halfway down Bow Lane. Tall, half-timbered with a tile roof and bay windows that looked out onto the street, the house was that of a wealthy family but not ostentatious, as Rich's house in Islington was. Will rapped on the door and a young woman answered. She was pretty - petite and thin - and blushed deeply when she saw Will. "Richard Rich sent me," Will said. "I am Will...," he paused momentarily. "Jones."

The girl curtseyed. "Master Jones," she said. "We have been expecting you. I am Philippa Jenkes. My cousin is engaged to Master Rich."

THE FAILED APPRENTICE

Will's eyes widened. So that was the connection. He bowed. "Pleased to meet you, Mistress."

Philippa stepped aside so Will could enter the house. The entrance was paneled in dark wood, and candles burned on small tables, casting flickering shadows on the walls. The floor was covered in rush mats, with meadowsweet cast upon them. When Will crossed into the front room, the herb gave off a flowery scent. He smiled to himself; he had used meadowsweet to alleviate his headaches after a night of hard drinking. This was clearly a more refined use of the herb.

An older woman rounded the corner wiping her hands on a dishrag. "Mistress Philippa, you should not be opening the door, especially if strange men are on the other side of it!" she scolded.

"Mistress Byrne," Philippa said. "You were in the cellar, and Master Jones was waiting. I hardly think he poses a threat."

"Oh, Master Jones!" Mistress Byrne said, swatting Philippa with the dishrag. "I am sorry you had to wait. But Mistress Philippa should not be opening our door. Too many evil people lurking about, don't you know."

Will smiled as he watched Mistress Byrne regard Philippa with a maternal, protective love. Then he thought of his own family, his father's abrupt dismissal of him and his quick condemnation of Amy. A knot formed in his stomach, which he tried to ignore.

Mistress Byrne showed Will to his room, a small chamber on the second floor. Philippa followed. "I am sorry this is not more luxurious," she said. "I am sure you are used to finer accommodations."

Rich had apparently not shared Will's background with his new landlords. Will resisted telling Philippa about the dungeon in the Tower, his filthy room on Bear Lane in Southwark, or his tiny closet at his family's home. Compared to these, this small chamber, with a comfortable bed, wood plank floor, glassed windows, and a nightstand that was not broken, was a treat.

Will ate with Philippa's family that evening in their cozy dining room. Philippa's father, John Jenkes, was a successful London grocer, and his wife, Maud, was from a family of physicians.

Although soft-spoken, John Jenkes' status was evident in the expensive furnishings throughout the dining room - a decoratively carved oak table, sturdy and cushioned chairs, and a green and gold tapestry of the Jenkes' coat of arms.

"Will, how do you know Master Rich?" John Jenkes asked, leaning forward, elbows on the table. Will looked at him closely, checking for a subtext, but there was none. Jenkes smiled. He had no clue as to Will's past.

"We are involved in some business dealings," Will said, as a slice of bread lodged in his throat, making him choke.

"Ah, we are fortunate Master Rich is in our lives and engaged to my niece Elizabeth," Maud Jenkes said. "He has been good to our family. He is such a kind man."

If you only knew, Will thought.

THE FAILED APPRENTICE

Chapter 13

The following day Will took a detour from Cheapside to Southwark. Amy had been on his mind, and he had no idea what Ellyn thought happened to him after Rich had him arrested. He needed to put their minds at ease.

Will's first stop was the Axe, which looked a bit more dilapidated from when Will was there last, even though it had been mere days. He walked in as Ellyn's voice echoed from the back: "I'll be right out with some fine girls!"

Ellyn emerged from the back room, saw Will, and rushed to embrace him. "I thought you were dead!" she said. "I thought Rich would have you hanged!"

"I'm alive," Will said, feeling his chest as if to make sure. "Although there was a time I wasn't sure I'd be."

Ellyn sighed in relief. "That arse Rich is more merciful than I thought," she said. "When can you come back to work?"

Will cleared his throat. "Unfortunately, I made a deal with Rich, which is the only reason I am still alive. I'm working for him now, although this is only a short-term job."

"Ah, then I was right. It's always tit for tat with him. I should have figured he'd work this to his advantage," Ellyn said. "I don't want to know what you'll be doing for him."

"Correct," Will said.

Ellyn laid an age-spotted hand on Will's arm. "Be careful, Will. I mean it. He's not a good man."

"I know," Will nodded.

"A right clinker but a powerful one. A dangerous combination."

"I am aware," Will replied. "I don't have much time, Ellyn. I need to go see Amy."

"You best. She's beside herself with worry. Nick was just here. He knows what happened, that you were arrested."

Will embraced Ellyn. "I'll try to get back to check on you."

"Don't worry about me. I'm tough."

Will laughed. Indeed she was.

Will left the Axe and continued down Bankend to Winchester Palace. As always, the palace filled Will with both awe and trepidation. It was so large, so grand, Will felt small, insignificant in its presence.

Will feigned an air of confidence and strode into the palace. Yet just after passing through the portico, he heard a voice call out, "You there!" A cold shiver ran down his spine. Perhaps he would end up swinging from a rope after all.

Will was about to turn and run just as he saw Nick smiling and striding toward him. "The look on your face!" he said. "Thank the Lord you are alive."

Will grasped Nick's forearm. "You scared me to death, you cur," he said. "It's so good to see a friendly face."

Nick smiled. "Ellyn told me about Rich. You weren't really stealing from him, were you?"

Will gulped. He wasn't *really* stealing; his hand had never actually extracted coins from the bag. "Of course not," he replied.

"I knew you wouldn't be so stupid. Ellyn said you were just moving his cloak."

Will nodded. Let Nick think what he wanted.

"So what happened? Rich let you off?"

"Essentially. But I did spend a night in the Tower. It was terrible, worse than you could imagine."

"I've heard pretty bad stories," Nick said. "I'm glad you made it out alive."

"Me too," Will said as the two moved deeper into the palace. "But I'm all right. But how's Amy?"

"Amy is thriving," Nick said. "See for yourself."

Amy stood at the far side of the hall, speaking with another chambermaid. She looked up, spied Will, and made a dash for him. "Will!" she said, embracing him. "I've been so worried about you! But look at you. You are dressed in all sorts of finery!"

"I had a short stint in the Tower; it was bad. But Rich had me released," he said. "He even helped me find a job."

THE FAILED APPRENTICE

"Incredible," Nick said. "I've heard Rich can be mean, vindictive. He must like you."

Will shrugged and looked at Amy. "What does Rich have you doing?" Amy asked.

"I'm just a messenger at the Mercers' Hall," Will said.

"That's good," Nick said. "I've heard he's caught up in all sorts of underhanded things."

"I wouldn't know about that," Will said. He turned and held Amy at arm's length. In the short time she had been at the palace, she had gained weight, and her skin was glowing. "Look at you," he said. "Amy, you look great."

Amy looked at Nick and smiled. "This is a good job, and I have Nick to thank for it. The work is not hard, and I am not living in fear of being attacked." Nick watched a look pass between Amy and Nick. Amy blushed, and Nick suppressed a smile. Well, Will thought. Then there's that.

"And Culler?" Will said. "Have you seen him?"

"He has not been around, and Ellyn will not allow him back at the Axe," Nick said.

"Good. Let's hope it remains as such," Will said. The three looked at each other, relief marking their faces, their worries lessened if only for a moment. Will sighed. "I best be going," he said, then handed Nick a slip of paper. "My address. I have a room on Bow Lane if you or Amy need me."

"Bow Lane?" Nick raised an eyebrow but said nothing.

"Bow Lane," Will said definitively. He hugged Nick and kissed Amy's forehead. "I can be here in moments."

The following month progressed much the same. Will served as a messenger for Dauntesey, reading documents on the sly and finding out nothing important. In his free time, he lurked around the hall, eavesdropping. But all he heard were merchants' complaints about their wives, the rising cost of ale, and how tired they were.

Rich was getting annoyed as well. "My patience is not infinite," he said to Will after another uneventful week. "Either you find me someone to hang, or you will find yourself on the gallows. I will not be played for a fool."

Although Will's life at the Mercers' Hall was becoming increasingly stressful, his life at the Jenkes' home had fallen into a pleasant routine. The Jenkes family was kind and generous with their home and time, sharing meals with Will and engaging him in conversation. And although John Jenkes never asked Will to contribute to his upkeep, Will passed along some of the coins he received as gratuities from his life as a courier.

And then there was Philippa. Will was intrigued by Philippa Jenkes but did not understand her. Whenever she was around Will, she blushed, looked at her feet, and could barely utter words without stammering. At first, Will thought she disliked him, but when Mistress Byrne pulled him aside and mentioned that Philippa was "sweet on him," Will was shocked. He was used to the brazen women of Southwark, the ones who hooted to Will as he walked by, who squeezed their breasts provocatively and ran their tongues over their lips, who asked Will to screw them "for free." Those women he could understand, those women he could deal with. Philippa was a different kind of woman entirely.

As winter waned and the days lengthened, Will and Philippa began to take strolls along the Thames before supper. Yet Philippa rarely initiated conversation, and Will found himself searching for things to talk about with this innocent girl. The deafening bells of St. Mary-le-Bow were a godsend; Will didn't have to work at conversation when they were ringing. Anything he said could not be heard over their clamoring.

One evening in March, Will and Philippa walked south toward the Thames. The breeze was soft, birdsong filling the air, and magpies foraged for twigs for their nests. Will took Philippa's hand in his. It was soft - a hand that had never seen labor, had never been slapped with a piece of leather, had never swatted away a rat. He looked at her eyes, blue and trusting, and leaned over to kiss her. He was surprised when she returned his kiss. He was sure she had never been kissed before, but her lips were gentle, welcoming, and responsive. He pulled back and touched

THE FAILED APPRENTICE

her face. She blushed but smiled; she trusted him implicitly. If he could only tell her his history, he thought. Yet she didn't even know his real last name.

Two weeks passed, and Rich was growing irritated with Will. That morning Will had approached a group of merchants at the hall and attempted to strike up a conversation. "I'm Will Jones," he said. "From Bristol." He emphasized Bristol, hoping to convey a knowledge of smuggling.

"Bristol?" One of the men said. "I once knew someone in Bristol. The most hilarious man I have ever met. Robert Richards, an attorney. Do you know him?"

"No," Will said.

"Your loss," the man said and turned his back to Will.

That afternoon Will met with Rich. "What are you doing over there?" he yelled, slamming his fist onto the table. "Making friends? You have one job - one job, you little cur - to do. Do it!"

"I'm trying," Will said. "It takes a while to build trust with the merchants."

"Trust?" Rich raged. He picked up a pewter tankard and hurled it at Will's head. Will dodged the projectile, but just barely. "You have two weeks to find me something, you stupid dolt."

"How am I supposed to find out anything?" Will asked. "They give me access to nothing other than meaningless lists."

"Is this *my* problem?" Rich said. "You aren't an idiot, although you're acting like one. I have no compunction in personally hauling you up on the the gallows and putting the noose around your neck myself!"

Will went to bed that night, but sleep eluded him. He thought of his final moments on the gallows, which seemed more and more likely to occur. Would Nick come to see Will lose his life? He hoped Amy would stay away. No one should see their brother face such a shameful death.

However, Will's luck changed the following day. Will began his morning as usual, lurking around the hall, eavesdropping, trying to develop a friendship or, at least, a connection. He approached a group of men who surrounded a boisterous one, his back turned to Will. "And then," the man boasted, "I threw the wench up against the wall and had her screaming with pleasure."

The men responded with general guffawing. But there was something familiar about the man - the size, the stance, the tufts of black hair, the grating quality of his voice. When the man turned sideways, Will recognized him immediately. It was Culler.

Culler spied Will, and Will felt a cold shiver pass over him. He tempered down his desire to attack Culler, to bash his head in, to take revenge for what he had done to Amy. But fear also passed through Will. All Culler had to do was to remember Will from the Axe, to call him out as an imposter. But Culler appeared to not recognize Will; why should he? To Culler, Will had been nothing more than a repairman at the Axe, no one to even acknowledge. Culler stood aside and invited Will into the circle of men. "I don't recognize you," Culler said. "You must be new."

"I am," Will managed to croak out. "I'm Will Jones. I'm learning from Master Dauntesey. My uncle is a merchant in Bristol."

Culler smiled. "Bristol, I know it well," he said, then chuckled and winked at Will. "I've done quite a share of business in Bristol. See this cloak?" He turned in a circle, the velvet billowing around his short frame, exposing the fur lining. "I can thank Bristol for this!"

"Impressive," Will said, remembering when he had tried on that very cloak. "Perhaps someday I can wear something just as fine."

Culler continued to brag about his ill-gotten wealth and his women until Will had heard enough. He excused himself and watched Culler from a distance, his blood running cold. The hubris of that man, Will thought. This is where it ends.

That evening Will sent a message to Rich. He had some information Rich might find interesting. The weeks of waiting had begun paying off.

The following day Will did not go to the Mercers' Hall but met Rich in Whitehall. As Will walked to Rich's chamber, he nearly bumped into a dark-haired, beady-eyed man striding purposefully in the other direction. "Excuse me, my lord," Will said as the man

THE FAILED APPRENTICE

shouldered past, but the man ignored him and kept going. Will turned and watched him move down the corridor. A palatable cloud of power surrounded him. As he approached, men turned away, fearful of being seen, or bowed their heads and avoided eye contact.

Will entered Rich's chamber. "You just missed Master Cromwell," Rich said.

"Cromwell?" Will replied. The name was unfamiliar to him.

Rich rolled his eyes. "Thomas Cromwell, the king's right hand. That man is going places, and I'm attaching myself to his rising star. You really don't get around much, do you?"

Will ignored the insult. "I have a name for you," he said. "A man deep into the smuggling business."

Rich leaned in. "Go on."

Chapter 14

Hugh Culler was hauled into the Court of the Exchequer the next day. Held at Westminster Hall, the court handled financial transgressions against the king, primarily focusing on smuggling. Once it was clear Culler was not going to weasel his way out of the indictment, two other merchants came forward to support the flimsy charge against him.

Will lingered in the back of the court, his heart hammering as he listened to the scant evidence against the man. Whether or not Culler was an actual smuggler was irrelevant to him. Culler had raped Amy, and it was for this crime he would pay.

It did not take long for a verdict to come down. Since smuggling eroded the royal finances and was an increasing problem, the judgment was harsh, and Culler would be made an example of. His actual guilt or innocence was inconsequential; King Henry needed a man to serve as a lesson to other would-be smugglers, and Culler was it. Stealing from the Crown would not be tolerated, and Culler seemed to fold in on himself as the guilty verdict was read. He was then grabbed by two burly court officers and hauled off to Newgate Prison, where he would await his fate.

Two weeks later, Will lingered outside Newgate. He arrived early; he wanted to see Culler as he was hauled from the prison and into an ox cart for the trip to the gallows at Tyburn. Will's eyes would not leave the man until he was swinging from the gibbet, his feet in soft calfskin shoes spastically grasping for purchase.

"I knew you'd be here," a voice next to Will said. Will looked to his left. It was Nick. "Divine justice for the sodding lecher."

"He was smuggling," Will said and then smiled. "Or so it seems."

Moments later, the door opened, and Culler was led out, his eyes squinting in the noonday sun, his hands tied in front of him, a noose loosely hanging around his neck. Following him was

THE FAILED APPRENTICE

another prisoner. From the other man's rags, it was clear that these two men were from very different social circles but would be taking their last ride together. While the raggedy prisoner leapt about and stuck his tongue out at the amassing crowds, Culler looked around frantically, hoping for someone to help him, come to his rescue, aid in an escape. But as the jailer loaded him into the cart and the first rotten tomato hit his fine velvet cape, he began to cry.

"Enough!" The jailer yelled at the crowd, straining to be heard over the bells of nearby St. Sepulcher, which had just begun to toll. "That cape's the hangman's payment after this filcher drops. Aim for the face, not the cape."

But as the cart began its three-mile journey, a fistful of shit hit Culler just below his neck. The cape was surely ruined now.

Will and Nick followed the cart, careful that the jostling onlookers did not knock them to the road or pick their pockets. As they moved down Snow Hill and across the bridge over the Fleet River, the crowds became larger and more boisterous. Onlookers leaned out of their windows as they passed, screaming at the condemned and throwing the contents of their chamber pots at the cart. Culler's cart mate blew kisses to the crowd; Culler stared blankly at his feet.

The cart lumbered through Holborn and St. Giles, stopping briefly at the church in St. Giles-in-the-Field. There, a churchman offered Culler and the other prisoner a bowl of ale, a final drink before meeting the hangman. The crowd had become swollen and loud, and Will and Nick forced their way in front of the cart. As they passed, Will looked at Culler, who was trying to pour the ale into his mouth with his bound hands. His cape was now encrusted with rotten fruit, mud, and excrement. Will felt no pity.

The walk from St. Giles to Tyburn was short. Many people skipped walking with the cart altogether and gathered around the gallows, jockeying for a prime viewing spot. Vendors milled about, selling food and drink. From the tenor of the mob, many had already had several pints of ale. "Watch your money," Nick said. "Pickpockets are everywhere."

Will laughed. "Money? That's one thing I don't have."

Will and Nick moved toward the wooden gallows, elbowing people out of the way. "Hey," one man said, his breath already reeking of drink. "I've been here for over an hour! I got here early for a good view. You best not be pushing past."

Nick looked at the man and laughed. "I am here under the direction of Bishop Gardiner. Take it up with him," he said.

The man's eyes widened, and he stepped back. "I don't want no trouble from Wily Winchester," he said, motioning for Will and Nick to pass.

Soon the cart holding Culler arrived and backed up under the gallows, people scattering out of the way. The hangman grabbed the rope around Culler's neck and tossed it up to his assistant, who sat, balanced, on the beam above the men. The assistant tied the rope to the gallows. "It's good and tight," he yelled to the hangman. "No one will be wiggling out of this."

The hangman did the same with the other prisoner, who had become even more energized during his cart ride to Tyburn. With his hands tied, the other prisoner danced about, pulled his trousers down, and began urinating on the crowd. "Let's get this over with," the executioner said. "This one's a showman."

Sensing the impending deaths, the crowd became so raucous that Will could not hear the prayers the priest was saying with the condemned men. He did not care. Prayers or not, Will was sure Culler was going to Hell, despite any last-minute confession or appeal to God. Then the hangman placed nightcaps over the men's heads, gave the signal, and the cart lurched away.

Will watched as Culler's feet tried to remain on sure footing, but soon he was flailing in the air, a short drop, not nearly enough to break his neck. A cheer swelled as both men's feet kicked, fruitlessly searching for solid ground. Soon, both men's legs relaxed, and urine and feces began dribbling down their legs. Nick nodded to Will. "A fitting end, covered in his own shit."

So that's done, Will thought. Amy can rest easy.

Will and Nick left Tyburn. Many onlookers remained, enjoying the food and drink, the camaraderie of watching the dead bodies

THE FAILED APPRENTICE

sway in the breeze. In an hour or so, Culler would be cut down, his clothes becoming the property of the hangman, his body claimed by his family or sent to the Surgeons' Hall to be dissected.

Will and Nick walked through Holborn back toward the center of London. It was midday, and the spring sun was warming. "Let's get a drink," Nick said. "There's something I would like to talk to you about."

After the crowds dissipated, the two men ducked into the Saracen's Head, an inn on Snow Hill catering to travelers since the Middle Ages. They found a small table that overlooked a large courtyard and ordered two tankards of ale. Will took a sip of ale and felt the enormity of the day wash over him. Culler was dead, in one of the most ignominious ways possible, hanging from the gallows with a common criminal, shit and piss staining his lifeless corpse, crowds jeering at him, his precious cape ruined. Amy had been avenged, and his deal with Rich was complete. A weight had been lifted from his shoulders.

"So," Nick said, staring into his tankard of ale. He took a long gulp, then looked at Will. "Amy."

"Amy," Will replied, enjoying Nick's discomfort.

Nick let out a loud sigh. "I am in love with her."

Will laughed. "That's obvious. But Amy? Does she feel the same?"

"She does," Nick said, his eyes dancing.

Will nodded. "I could tell when I saw you both at the palace. Neither of you was very good at hiding it."

"I wanted to make sure you are fine with this," Nick said.

"I am," Will replied. "But isn't this awfully fast? It's been what, just a few months?"

Nick waved his hand dismissively in front of his face. "It was an immediate thing, you know? For both of us." Nick grinned.

"So it seems."

"Do you think I should approach her father?" Nick said. "Ask his permission to court his daughter, and all that?"

Will took a long pull on his ale. "I am happy Amy has found someone. You, actually." Will laughed. "But I would not go to my parents. Since the incident with Culler, Amy is not welcome in their home. They think she is a thief, someone who didn't appreciate her position."

"I thought as much," Nick said. "We will muddle through without their blessing."

Will paused for a moment. "Do you intend to marry her?"

"I do. Not right now. But soon." Nick leaned back in his chair. "But I do have a confession."

Oh no, Will thought. Please do not let her be pregnant. "What?" he said. "This better not be what I think it is."

Nick's eyes became wide. "Lord, no. I was going to say that she is terrible at being a chambermaid. The other maids follow in her wake and clean up after her."

"Then best you marry her fast before she ends up on the street!"

"She is something, Will. She turns up her nose at the chamber pots and walks right over messes on the floor as if she doesn't see them. But everyone loves her. She is funny and friendly. She has a heart of gold."

"That's how she has always been," Will replied. "Just as long as you know your home will never be spotless."

"I have made peace with that," Nick said, laughing.

Will looked at Nick, who was beaming. He had not known Nick long, but he sensed he was a good man, a hard worker, who - most likely because of his pock-marked face - had not had a lot of luck with women. "Just treat her right," Will said.

"You know I will." The men clicked their tankards together. It had been a good day for him and for Nick and, by proxy, Amy.

Philippa was waiting for Will when he returned to the Jenkes' home later that afternoon. Although Will was exhausted, Philippa seemed eager for a walk before the evening meal. Will changed his clothes, and he and Philippa began their usual stroll toward the Thames.

THE FAILED APPRENTICE

"What did you do today?" Philippa ventured. Will was surprised; rarely did Philippa initiate conversation. More times than not, Will had to work just to pull a few sentences from her.

Will chose his words carefully. He could not tell Philippa he went to see his sister's rapist hanged, that he felt nothing but relief at the man's death. She looked up at him with expectant eyes. "I saw my friend Nick," Will said. "He is in love with my sister."

"I did not know you had a sister," Philippa said.

There's a lot you don't know about me, Will thought. Including my real name, my affiliation with Rich, my time in the Tower, my work at the Axe. He looked at Philippa. She was small, ivory-skinned, her dark hair curled and piled into a white lace bonnet, her cape a deep blue, delicate and unspoiled. Will thought of Nick, of the sparkle in his eyes when he talked about Amy. A union with Philippa would be good for Will; her family was wealthy and connected, and she was sweet and kind. She would be a good wife. But what kind of relationship was built on lies? And where was the spark Will longed for?

Will cut the walk short, and when they returned to the Jenkes' home, Mistress Byrne hurried to Will. "That unpleasant Angus left this for you," she said, handing Will a letter sealed with Rich's imprint. "That man is as mean as he is ugly."

Will took the letter and broke the seal. He read Rich's scrawl; Rich wanted to see him the next morning in Smithfield. Will smiled. Now he would be released from Rich's clutches. He could return to the Axe or, perhaps, continue at the Mercers' Hall in a legitimate capacity. "Is that from Master Rich?" Philippa asked.

"It is," Will replied.

"Such a lovely man," Philippa said.

Chapter 15

Will walked the short distance from Bow Lane to Smithfield the next morning. It was a beautiful spring day; the air was clean, and the breeze was soft. Will felt lighter. After handing Rich Culler, he was certain his fortunes were about to change.

Smithfield was teeming with people when Will arrived, and his heart dropped when he saw the familiar pyre set up in the center of the square, kindling stacked next to it. For a terrible moment, he feared the stake was meant for him, but then he saw Rich standing in the shade of a tree far from the execution site. Rich motioned for Will to come over. When Will cut his way through the crowd, he turned to Rich. "What's this?" he asked.

"Just a little lesson for you," Rich said. "Something I think you should see. I will meet with you tomorrow and explain. But today, I want you to see this. Stay here with me. It's best if we remain on the sidelines."

Shortly thereafter, the throng parted, and a middle-aged man, bearded and broken, was dragged to the pyre. "This man," Rich said, motioning to the prisoner, "is James Bainham. He was once a respected lawyer. In fact, I practiced with him at Middle Temple. He had a keen mind."

Will looked on, horrified, as chains were fastened around Bainham's body and the kindling moved to cover his feet and lower legs. "What did he do?" Will finally asked.

"Bainham dared speak out against the old faith, the papacy, the infallibility of Rome. Thomas More, the Lord Chancellor? He had Bainham arrested for heresy. Imprisoned him in his house in Chelsea, tied him to a tree on his property, and flogged him for his Protestant beliefs, which More deems as heretical." Rich cocked his head in the direction of the dais.

Will followed Rich's eyes and saw Thomas More sitting on the same platform where he had been during Richard Bayfield's

THE FAILED APPRENTICE

execution. More sported the same severe and inscrutable expression as he had those months before.

Rich sighed and continued. "Eventually, Bainham renounced his beliefs and was fined £20. But less than a month later, he recanted. More had him imprisoned in the Tower and racked, whipped. But Bainham would not denounce his beliefs. What you see now is the result of this. This is what happens when the old faith is threatened by the new."

Bainham, chained, watched as a court official carrying a torch approached. His eyes scanned the crowd, and then, in a voice surprisingly loud and clear, he announced: "I come accused and condemned for a heretic, Sir Thomas More being my accuser and my judge."

Will looked over at More, whose eyes narrowed. A cry went up from the assemblage: "Set fire to him and burn him!"

The kindling was ignited, and the flames began to crack and leap, first slowly but then with more vigor. Yet Bainham's face remained peaceful. Absent was the writhing and moaning Will had witnessed at Bayfield's execution. As the fire worked its way up Bainham's shattered body, he looked out at the assemblage and uttered, "You papists look for miracles, and now you may see a miracle. I feel no more pain than if I were in a bed of down." With that, a large flame rose above his head and consumed him, and Bainham was no more.

Will's eyes moved back to More, whose face was inscrutable. No emotion played on his lips; no satisfaction glimmered from his eyes. Will turned to Rich. "Why did I need to see this?"

"Come to my chamber tomorrow at 9:00," Rich said. "Don't be late." Rich turned and disappeared into the crowd leaving Will alone and confused, the smell of burning flesh lingering in the air.

The following morning was dark and rainy. When Will arrived at Whitehall, he was drenched. He shook his head like a dog coming in from a deluge.

Will knocked on Rich's door, aware of the rain dripping from his soaked clothing. "Come in," Rich yelled. Will entered. Rich sat behind his ornate desk, a quill in one hand and parchment in the other. "You are soaked," he said. "Don't go dripping on the chairs."

Will took off his cloak and hung it on a coat rack by the door. Although thin, the cloak had kept the worst of the rain from him. Will perched on a chair across from Rich, careful to keep the wetness from his breeches away from the fabric. "Here I am," he said. "As requested."

"Indeed you are." Rich put his quill and paper on his desk and moved to cover the writing with a piece of cloth.

"Why did I have to witness Bainham's execution yesterday? Was that a threat?"

"No threat, Will. I'll get to that in a minute." Rich tented his hands and leaned forward on the desk. "First, Culler. You did a good job with that."

"Thank you," Will replied.

"That should slow the smuggling, anyway. A good lesson for common thieves." Rich sat back and appraised Will. "I have another assignment for you."

"What?" Will said. "I thought we were even. I got you your smuggler. I was told I'd be left alone once this was done."

"Yes, well…" Rich said. "That's not what's going to happen."

"And if I refuse?" Will said, knowing that refusal was not really an option. He remembered Bainham at the pyre. Perhaps this was a threat after all.

Rich laughed. "You won't refuse. I still have you for attempted theft."

Will shut his eyes. There was no recourse.

"Oh, stop whining," Rich said. "This is good for you. Think of it as career advancement. What were you going to do anyway? Go back to the Axe?"

"Very well," Will said. "What is it?"

Rich smiled. "There's about to be a big shakeup at court. Thomas More is expected to refuse to agree to the Submission of the Clergy. This will be bad for him. Very bad indeed."

"What's the Submission of the Clergy?" Will asked.

THE FAILED APPRENTICE

"You really don't know anything, do you?" Rich scoffed. "The Submission gives King Henry power over the church. The church will no longer be separate from the Crown, effectively making King Henry head of the church. More has been outspoken in his rejection of this. You know what a fanatic he is. You saw it yourself yesterday."

"I know nothing about church politics," Will said. "I'm probably not the best choice for this assignment."

"And you knew nothing about being a merchant, either. Yet you led us to Culler dancing on the gibbet."

"So who do you want me to spy on this time? One of Thomas More's lackeys?"

Rich laughed. "You need to have a bit more confidence, my young friend. Cromwell's sights are set on More himself. Therefore, mine are too. More and the king are on a collision course. If I can help bring More down, I'll raise myself all the higher. But even more than that, Cromwell doesn't like him. Which means I don't either."

"Thomas *More*?" Will's eyes widened and his throat tightened. This obviously involved more than hanging around the Mercers' Hall. Will shook his head. "No."

Rich waved a dismissive hand at Will. "I have deep connections, Will. Wheels within wheels. I've arranged for you to move in with More's family in Chelsea. He has hired several young men as tutors. We have found you a placement to teach two of his young grandchildren. They are More's daughter Margaret Roper's brats. Girls. More seems to think it's good for women to be educated." Rich rolled his eyes.

"Tutor? Tutor these girls in what? Deceit?"

"You can read, you dumbarse. Teach them their letters. They're little girls; they don't need much. Give them a hornbook. Your real job is to keep your eyes and ears on More."

Will and Rich stared at each other for a moment. "What am I to be looking for?"

"Anything More says against the church - the reformed church, the church of Henry VIII. Any conversation critical of the king or his mistress Anne Boleyn. Any support of Queen Katherine. It's all treasonous now."

"This plan is outrageous," Will finally said.

"It's outrageous only in its brilliance." Rich sat back and grinned. "This is a long-term assignment. I don't expect you to uncover much right away. Take your time and gain More's confidence. Ask probing questions, gain his trust. Then we strike."

Will shook his head. Rich was clearly delusional. "This won't work," he said.

"Listen," Rich said. "More can be kind. Charming. He can be good to those he deems worthy. I showed you Bainham's burning yesterday because I want you to remember what Thomas More is about. Fanaticism. Adherence. Punishment. Death. Do not be lulled into a soft life in Chelsea. Remember what you have seen."

Will shook his head. "This is too much for me," he said. "I can't do this."

"I am giving you a horse," Rich said, ignoring Will. "You need to be able to get back and forth from Chelsea. It's outside. Angus is looking after it."

"A *horse*?"

Rich looked at Will and sighed. "This is how I see it, Will. You are a young man who has no real tether to anything and owes me a favor. I am a man with ambition and connections. I see big changes coming to court, and I intend to play them to my advantage. You would be smart to attach your fortunes to mine. We can help each other."

Will had to admit Rich had a plan. Will had nowhere to go, that was clear. He could ride it out at Chelsea for as long as he needed. He would just keep out of More's way.

"Oh, and break it off with Philippa," Rich said. "Tell John Jenkes you need to return to Bristol. That should end it. She is a pretty little thing, though." Rich winked at Will.

Of course, Rich knew about Philippa. Will ignored the directive. "When am I supposed to go to Chelsea?"

"You're expected at the end of the week."

THE FAILED APPRENTICE

"And am I still going by Will Jones?"

Rich smiled. "I think we are done with Jones. You can return to your given surname. I can't remember what it is."

"Patten," Will said.

"Of course. Now go."

Will left Whitehall and spied Angus on the street, holding the reins of a young piebald hobby. The horse eyed Will and stomped its foot. "Saved this one especially for you," Angus said with a sneer, the scar on his face puckering. "Good luck." He handed Will the reins and disappeared into Whitehall.

Will turned to the horse. "Do you have a name?" he asked. The horse bared his teeth.

Will climbed onto the horse's saddle. It was old, with deep marks in the leather, but the wear made the saddle soft. The horse bucked and snorted, Will pulled back on the reins, and the horse settled. "I'll call you Baucent," he said. "It's a knight's war cry. And you are obviously looking for a fight."

Will finally got Baucent under control and rode the short distance to Bow Lane. He guided Baucent to a small stable behind the Jenkes' home and handed the reins to a tired-looking stableboy. "He's got an attitude," Will said. "Be careful." The stableboy laughed, but when Baucent moved to kick him, he yelped and leapt out of the way.

Over supper, Will told John Jenkes that he would be leaving by week's end. "I will be moving back to Bristol," he lied. "You have been more than generous with your hospitality. If I can ever help you, please let me know. You can get ahold of me through Master Rich."

Philippa looked at Will, her eyes filling with tears. "Excuse me," she said and ran from the table.

John Jenkes leaned forward. "We are all sorry to see you go." He paused. "Especially Philippa. I had hoped that you two would marry. She is clearly taken with you, and you're an upstanding young man. I would be proud to have you as a son, Master Jones."

"Philippa is a lovely girl," Will said. His stomach began twisting in knots. Then, as close as he dared get to the truth: "I think she can deserves a better man than me."

"But would you consider it?" Jenkes continued. "We can have a betrothal. Distance should not be a factor. She can move to Bristol with you."

How could Will break this girl's heart? She was so innocent, so naive. "I am sorry, Master Jenkes. I cannot."

"Do you have a woman in Bristol?" Jenkes asked, sighing.

Will shook his head. "It's nothing like that. It's just," his mind whirled, trying to come up with a believable lie. "My father wants me to wed a colleague's daughter. I have not met the girl, but my father seems insistent." He hoped the lie would end the discussion. "I would be proud to have Philippa as a wife, but I am in a bit of a mess in Bristol."

"Very well," John Jenkes said. "But if that doesn't work out, let me know. This is something Philippa won't get over quickly."

"I will," Will said. "And I would be honored to be a part of your family. If only things were different." This, he meant.

THE FAILED APPRENTICE

Chapter 16

By the end of the week, Will was ready to leave London. He sent letters to Nick, Amy, and Ellyn indicating that he could be found at More's home in Chelsea. Notes were better, Will thought. No one could question him as to why he was spending time at Thomas More's house. No one could corner him in a lie that could come back to bite him.

Will mounted Baucent and began the trip to Chelsea, his small pack of belongings secured to the saddle. As he rode away from the house on Bow Lane, he looked back and saw Philippa standing at an upstairs window, watching him go. Perhaps he had made a mistake, perhaps he should have figured a way to marry Philippa - John Jenkes might understand if Will carefully explained his ruse, but chances are he wouldn't. And Philippa deserved better than that.

Will rode south, then followed the Thames westward, past Westminster, and out of London. Once the noise of the city diminished, Baucent calmed and seemed to sense a purpose to the trip. As the pair moved away from London, the road turned from cobblestone to dirt. Houses became scarcer and grander, and rolling meadows and spring flowers sweetened the air. Sheep grazed under sprawling oaks. As Will breathed in the fresh air, he felt his heartbeat slow.

Will knew how to get to Thomas More's home. Rich had scribbled directions on the back of a receipt, and Will had memorized them. It wasn't a difficult ride, and when he saw a massive red-brick home with two gatehouses leading to two courtyards, manicured gardens, a private quay, and flowering orchards, he knew he had arrived.

Will loosely tethered Baucent to a nearby post and walked up the serpentine path to the front door. A large mulberry tree cast a shadow on the walkway, and Will remembered Rich's words about Bainham tethered to a tree and flogged. Surely it wasn't this mulberry that stood in public view? Will wondered how a house this grand, surrounded by the soft scents of rosemary and lavender, could harbor such a tyrant.

Will mounted three stone steps to the porch curtained in jasmine and honeysuckle, intoxicated by the smell, the only sound that of bees drunk on nectar. Before knocking on the vast, wooden door, he breathed deeply. He knew he was at More's for less than a forthright purpose, yet he felt calm, peaceful. Everything about the grand home spoke of quietude and beauty. Will picked up the iron knocker and let it fall, emitting a noise that resounded throughout the house. Moments later, a matron opened the door, a warm smile on her round face. Will bowed. "I am Will Patten," he said. "I am to tutor the Lord Chamberlain's granddaughters."

"Ah, Master Patten, yes," the chambermaid said. She craned her neck past Will to view his horse grazing near the door. "Take your horse to the stables behind the house. Then come in through the back door. I'll tell the mistress you are here."

Will took Baucent, who had calmed significantly since leaving London, to the stables and handed him off to a young stablehand. The groom looked questioningly at the horse and at Will. "This piebald yours?" he said.

"He is," Will said. Then, as an afterthought, "He's a good horse."

"He's got a battle scar," the man said, pointing to a jagged mark along Baucent's neck. Will hadn't noticed that before. "By the looks of it, it was a nasty wound." The groom eyed Will with suspicion.

"I just got him," Will said. "I don't know his history."

"Something like that can spook a horse, make him scared. Or mean."

So that explained Baucent's earlier aggression. Will wondered if Angus had something to do with that. "Then be gentle with him," Will said, rubbing the horse's back. Baucent's tail swished, but he remained calm.

THE FAILED APPRENTICE

"I'll be good to him, you can be sure. I'm the best groom Sir Thomas has. Just ask anyone. My name's Rory; my whole family works for the Mores."

Will thanked Rory and turned toward the house. He took his time as he walked through the kitchen garden, the buzzing of bees merging with birdsong, the fragrance of blooms dispelling London's smell and the Thames' filth. The back door was half the size of the door at the front of the manor but was still sturdy and impressive. Will knocked, and the same matron opened it. "Come in, Master Patten," she said. "My name is Mistress Woolley, but everyone calls me Mags. The mistress is in the hall."

Will followed Mags down the long corridor to a great hall, a massive room over seventy feet long with a soaring beamed ceiling and large oriel windows. At the end of the room stood a raised dais. At the other end was a large stone fireplace. More's wife sat at a virginal in the corner next to the hearth.

Alice More, Thomas More's second wife, was a stout woman abutting the end of middle age. Although not beautiful, she was formidable, with dark hair pulled tightly under a black and gold mantle, large dark eyes, and thin lips. Two dogs slept at her feet while she plunked out a tune with her index fingers on the ivory keyboard. She looked up at Will and laughed. "I am just learning the virginal. My husband suggested I need something to keep my substantial nose out of his business. Do you play?"

Will looked at the virginal, a beautiful keyboard instrument constructed of dark wood gilded with scrolls and roses. "I wish I did," he said. He reached his hand out to touch the smooth wood. It was cool under his fingertips.

"Well then, Tutor Will, perhaps I can teach *you* a thing or two."

Will bowed. "Lady More."

"You will be responsible for teaching my granddaughters, Lizzy and Meg Roper. Little hellcats they are, don't let them fool you. Thomas has had to lash them on more than one occasion."

Will's eyes widened, but Alice More laughed. "My husband beats the girls with peacock feathers," she said. "My husband is a poor disciplinarian."

Will remembered Bayfield, Bainham, and the others who had met their end at the pyre on orders of More. He wondered if Alice was aware of the fates of these men.

"You will find this to be a busy household. We eat together - family, servants, and visitors. We share ideas, debate issues. You will not want for company. Or intellectual stimulation." Alice looked Will up and down. "I hope you are not shy."

Will laughed. "I've never been accused of shyness."

"Very well." Alice More stood up and smoothed her skirts. "Mags!" she yelled, her mouth opening wider than Will thought possible. Will jumped at the outburst, surprised at how such a loud noise could emit from such a refined woman. "Mags!" Alice More bellowed again. Moments later, Mistress Woolley raced into the room, wiping her hands on her apron.

"Mags, show Will his room," Alice More said. "And feed him. He's scrawny."

Will bowed and followed Mags as they left the great hall and headed to the west side of the house opposite the hall. After snaking through a well-stocked pantry, kitchen, and buttery, they mounted a staircase less grand than the one in the great hall but still more impressive than the creaky, uneven stairs on Fenn Road.

The top of the staircase opened to a corridor from which many small rooms branched off. Mags led Will to the door closest to the stairs and opened it. "This room is yours," she said. "You're in the servants' wing. This is probably the best room amongst all the rooms on this corridor. You have quite a view."

Will expected a small room, like his garret at Topside's or his closet on Fenn Road. By comparison, this room was spacious, with an elevated bed covered in a down coverlet, a desk and chair, and an oak trunk for storage. A rectangular mullioned window overlooked a sprawling, flowering orchard. From beyond the orchard, Will noticed two outbuildings that resembled smaller replicas of More's grand manor.

"Take time to settle in," Mags said. "I'll send some food up. Supper is at 7:00."

"Thank you, Mistress Woolley."

THE FAILED APPRENTICE

"It's Mags. I don't go for formalities." Mags smiled at Will, turned, and left.

Moments later, a small tray of fruit appeared, which Will devoured. He changed clothes, washed his face, and unpacked his small traveling sack, storing his few belongings in the trunk. As the light faded from his window, sounds began emanating up the stairs. He figured it was probably close to 7:00 and made his way to supper. A knot began forming in his stomach. How would Thomas More respond to him?

But Will need not have worried. The great hall was full of people, but Thomas More was not one of them. Alice More, seated at the head table, motioned to Will. On her lap, she held a squirming, dark-haired girl. "Let me go!" the child demanded.

"Will," Alice said. "This is Meg Roper, one of the two wild beasts you will be teaching. Meg, say hello to your new tutor."

"I said, let me go!" Meg screamed as she twisted out of Alice's lap and ran to join a group of other children. Alice shrugged. "I wish you luck with that one," she said, shaking her head.

"She is certainly spirited," Will said. Then, "Is the Lord Chancellor here? I would be honored to meet him."

"He's at Whitehall for the week," Alice said. "He's staying in London. You will have time for him later. I'm sure he'll be talking your ears off soon."

Will smiled. That was the plan.

Will sat at a long trestle table well below the dais on which the family sat. Alice More remained at the center of the long table, surrounded by More's children, their spouses, and grandchildren. Two little girls - he believed them to be Lizzy and Meg - took turns smacking each other with their spoons. Finally, Lizzy reached over and yanked a handful of Meg's hair. Meg let out a howl and punched Lizzy in the arm. Will thought of his brothers John and Mark, their similar antics. His heart contracted, missing his parents and his siblings. But he quickly shook off that feeling. He was not welcome at his home. And he had a job to do.

Moments later, Alice More stood, and the room quieted. She cleared her throat and read a passage of Scripture; by the looks of things, this was an evening ritual. When Alice More was finished, she closed her book of Scripture and cleared her throat. "Before we begin our supper, please welcome Will Patten to our home," she said, pointing across the room at Will. All eyes turned to stare. "Will, please stand." On shaky legs, Will pulled himself up to his full height, heat rising from his chest to his cheeks. "Master Patten will be Meg and Lizzy's tutor," Alice continued. "God help him."

Will's eyes quickly canvassed the room. The Mores' household was large, and he felt many eyes sizing him up. Just before he sat, his gaze lighted on a young woman sitting to the side of the dais. Her hair was piled into a gabled hood, tendrils of blonde peeking out. She looked at Will and smiled, then turned away. Will felt a bolt of energy surge through him, and, for a moment, his breath left his body. Will plunked himself back onto the bench, startled by his reaction to this stranger. Food was served, but his appetite was gone. He spoke politely to those around him but had difficulty concentrating over the pounding of his heart. After the meal, Will stood, searching the room for the woman. But she was gone.

The following morning Will met Lizzy and Meg in a small room off the great hall, which served as their classroom. Will would teach the girls daily during the week, focusing on their letters and numbers. The afternoons were his to spend as he wished.

Will arrived in the little chamber before the girls. He had two hornbooks, one for each girl, and would start with that. While waiting, Will walked to the window and looked out on More's gardens. It was mid-May, and everything was in bloom. He saw a cook gathering herbs from the kitchen garden. She stood and swatted away a bee.

Moments later, the sounds of feet running through the corridor and children's laughter caused him to turn to the door. Lizzy and Meg barreled in, tripping over their skirts. Behind him was the woman he had seen last night. Once again, his breath caught in his throat.

"Master Patten, I'm delivering your charges," she said. "They are a bit wild this morning. Mags slipped them some marzipan."

THE FAILED APPRENTICE

"It's Will," Will said, staring inanely at the woman. He tried to speak, but his mouth had gone dry.

"Will," the woman said and curtseyed. "I'm Phoebe Houghton, their governess."

"Phoebe," Will said, continuing to stare. Phoebe Houghton was the most captivating woman Will had ever seen. She was tall, with a sharp nose than lips thin. Will felt his cheeks grow hot.

Phoebe watched Will stare at her, waiting for him to say something. When it was clear that Will was done speaking, Phoebe said, "I'll be back in a bit. Good luck with the girls." She turned and left.

Embarrassed, Will turned his attention to More's granddaughters. Both were jumping up and down and screaming. Any hope of having them concentrate on letters or numbers was fading quickly.

"Do you know your alphabet?" Will asked.

"We're not stupid," Lizzy said. "We know our ABCs."

"I'm glad you're not stupid," Will said. "I was scared you both were doltheads."

Both girls stopped jumping and looked, slack-jawed, at Will. Then they started to laugh. "We're not *doltheads*, either!" Meg said.

"Idiots?" Will asked.

"Not idiots!" Lizzy said, laughing.

"Nincompoops?"

By now, both girls were doubled over laughing. "He said poop!" Meg screamed.

Will knew his plans with the hornbook would be wasted that day. Instead, he took the girls outside into the garden. "Find something beginning with the letter "A,"" Will said as Lizzy and Meg raced off to fulfill their assignment. These girls would clearly not sit still and embrace recitation and rote learning. He would need to be creative.

By the end of the morning, the girls had found items beginning with the letters A through L. They would finish the rest of the alphabet the next day. Phoebe found them in the garden, Lizzy clutching a lavender stem, Meg trying to hang on to a lizard. "Phoebe, look at our L's!" Meg said as the lizard leapt from her outstretched hand and scampered away.

"You actually got them to do something," Phoebe said to Will. "We can't keep a tutor. The girls are right terrors. But they seem to listen to you."

Will smiled. "I have brothers the same age," he croaked. "They can't sit still either."

Meg walked over to Phoebe and hung on her skirts. "I'm tired," she said as she yawned and rubbed her eyes.

"You are a miracle worker," Phoebe said. "This one is never tired." Then she addressed Meg. "Let's have a lie-down before our meal," she said. "Lizzy, you too."

"Goodbye, you nincompoop!" Lizzy said as she turned and waved at Will. Phoebe's eyes grew large. "Elizabeth Roper," she said. "We do not speak to people like that!" But behind the admonishment, Phoebe grinned.

The next several days passed in the same manner. When the weather was good, the girls played outside, Will forcing a little knowledge in. When the weather was poor, he made a game out of learning in their small classroom. It did not take long for him to realize the girls were smart, if undisciplined.

Will's interactions with Phoebe remained elusive, though. He stammered when she dropped off the girls and stammered some more when she picked them up. He lingered outside the nursery to no avail and stood around, self-conscious, before and after meals. Yet Phoebe Houghton failed to engage with Will. Each evening he went to bed, his heart heavy, another day no closer to getting to know the mysterious woman who plagued his thoughts.

Several days later, Will was walking in the orchards after the girls' lessons. The air was thick with humidity, the sun warming apple and cherry blossoms, the air heady with fragrance. Will was lost in thought - how could he get Phoebe alone? How could he keep from acting like, as Lizzy would say, a nincompoop in her presence?

THE FAILED APPRENTICE

Will heard the hoofbeats before he saw the horses arrive. A great cloud of dust surrounded a small group of riders as they turned onto More's lane and galloped to the stables. Will moved closer. Five men dismounted and shook the dust from their capes. Two were tall, two were short, and one emanated power. It was Thomas More.

Will had only seen Thomas More twice, both at the executions he had orchestrated. Now Will regarded him in a wholly new context. More moved easily with his men, although he was stooped and seemed to have a defeated air about him. Will followed More up the path leading to the house, keeping a safe distance and using the orchard trees as camouflage. It reminded Will of another time, a lifetime ago, when he followed Topside down the darkened London streets. The night when Topside disappeared into the Thames and Will's life changed forever. Perhaps the arrival of More heralded another such change.

More and his friends walked to the house and disappeared inside, leaving Will lingering on the outskirts of the orchard. Now his real work would begin.

Chapter 17

That night, the evening meal was especially chaotic. More was back, bringing four men with him. Alice More was clearly preoccupied. More's children seemed stoic. Only Lizzy and Meg seemed unfazed as they ran around the dais and tried to scramble onto More's lap.

More began the meal by reading a passage from Scripture. His voice was surprisingly low, and Will strained to hear what was being said. As supper was served, the man next to Will, one of More's personal servants named John Wood, leaned into Will. "Big doings at court, eh?" he said conspiratorially.

As usual, Will had no idea what was going on. "What do you mean?" he asked.

"More's back, and it isn't good," Wood said. "He refused to sign the king's Submission of the Clergy. He refused to acknowledge King Henry as head of the church. He has resigned his office as Lord Chancellor."

"What?" Will said, incredulous. "He resigned the Chancellorship?"

"He did. At first, the king refused to accept the resignation. They've been friends for a long time. But now, there's too much division between More and the king. More began suffering chest pains," Wood gripped his chest in sympathy. "The king relented and accepted More's resignation. It's a sad day, Will. At one time, More and King Henry were like brothers."

So Rich was right, Will thought. He saw this coming.

"I'm not clear as to why the king wants to be head of the church," Will ventured. "Isn't that the Pope's job?"

"Yes," John said. "If you follow the true Catholic Church, then the Pope is the head. But the Pope won't grant the king a divorce, which the king is desperate for. Hence, the break with the church. So now the king can set his own rules and get the divorce he wants. And marry the that Boleyn woman."

THE FAILED APPRENTICE

Will had heard of Anne Boleyn, the daughter of ambitious nobility who was educated in France and returned to King Henry's court to serve as a lady-in-waiting for Queen Katherine. She was reputed to be intelligent, charming, and manipulative. King Henry had fallen for her, and because Queen Katherine had failed to produce a male heir and was approaching the end of her childbearing years, Henry saw his chance for an heir with a new, young wife. Katherine had been cast aside, and Anne had almost effortlessly stepped into her place. All that remained was for the divorce to be granted, a wedding to take place, a baby boy to be conceived.

"Sir Thomas called his family together after he returned from London," John continued. "The king left him without an income from the court. Sir Thomas told his family that his income was now reduced, and they should help with the cost of running the household."

Will felt his stomach drop. Perhaps he would be relieved of his tutoring and spying duties? What would Rich do to him then?

"Don't worry, Will," John said. "Alice More is a wealthy woman. And Sir Thomas has a lot of income from rent and his other properties. The family will not end up in debtors' prison. And your job is secure."

Will exhaled. "Thank God for that," he said. "I just got here!"

"And Phoebe isn't going anywhere, either." John winked at Will, who looked horrified. "I've seen you gape at her. She's a fine-looking woman. If I was a decade or two younger, well..." he snickered.

"It's that obvious?' Will said. "How embarrassing."

"Well, yes." John laughed. "Just try to keep your tongue in your mouth when she's around."

Over the following days, Will tried to get close to More, but More spent most of his time holed up with either his wife, daughter Margaret Roper, or his advisors. Even Lizzy and Meg were more subdued and allowed themselves to be taught from Will's hornbook.

Several days later, after Will finished with the Roper girls' lessons, he was surprised to see Nick lingering outside the small classroom. "Nick," Will said, panic passing over him. "Is Amy all right?"

Nick embraced his friend. "Amy's fine. Bishop Gardiner is here to see More. I was asked to accompany him. I wanted to see you, so I agreed."

Will sighed in relief. "Let's walk," he said. "I'll show you the gardens. They're beautiful, and we can have some privacy."

Will and Nick left More's manor and walked through the kitchen gardens, which led to the orchards. "What are you doing here?" Nick asked.

"I'm tutoring Margaret Roper's girls. As you know."

Nick looked askance at Will. "No, what are you *really* doing here, Will? I don't buy the tutoring story."

Will shook his head. "Best you don't know. All I can say is that it involves Rich. I can't seem to shed him."

"Rich is little more than Thomas Cromwell's lapdog," Nick said, shaking his head.

"He still has power over me," Will said. "I wish I could get away from him."

"He's moving closer to Cromwell, I can tell you that," Nick said. "Cromwell has a list of those who oppose the king, practicing Catholics, papists. He passes the names on to Rich and most of them end up in the Tower. The man has no morals."

"Clearly," Will said. "If he did, I wouldn't be here."

In the distance, More walked with Stephen Gardiner, both men deep in conversation. They were far enough away that Will couldn't hear their words, but through their gestures he could tell the discussion was intense. "You obviously know More is no longer Lord Chancellor," Will said, motioning to the pair ahead.

"I do. That's why Bishop Gardiner is here. He and More are allies, and the king is angry with them both. Like More, Gardiner resisted the Submission, and now there are calls to strip Bishops of their power to hold a synod without permission from the king.

THE FAILED APPRENTICE

Can you imagine? Any merchant has the power to freely assemble - but not the clergy. That's not right."

Will shook his head. "What's driving this nonsense?"

Nick shrugged. "Anne Boleyn. The divorce. The king's inability to control the Pope. Thomas Cromwell. There are a lot of players in this, a lot of factions. I worry that Gardiner, in the end, will be a victim of his faith. He's conflicted. He's trying to straddle both worlds and not doing a great job of it."

Will nodded. "You have been to court," he said. "What's Anne Boleyn like?"

"Amy is much prettier," Nick said, smiling. "But Anne Boleyn is intelligent and charming. She leads the king around by the nose, and no one dare say a word against her. She doesn't like Gardiner; that is worrisome."

"I've never been a religious man," Will said. "I go to church as required. But these martyrs? These men who face the fire and the rack? I don't understand it. Certainly, God doesn't want a man to throw his life away at the hand of zealots."

Nick sighed. "We should not suppose we know what God wants. But these are confusing times. It's hard to know what's right and what will put you in the Tower or chained to the stake at Smithfield."

The two walked in silence, moving deeper into the orchards, approaching More's two outbuildings. Up ahead, More and Gardiner ducked into More's private chapel. "That's More's chapel," Will said, pointing at the small building. "The other is his library. I've been in neither. Since More returned from London, he spends a great deal of time in his chapel. I think he's looking for spiritual guidance."

Will and Nick turned and headed toward the Thames. "So," Nick said, rubbing his palm with his thumb. "I have some news. News that doesn't involve More or Gardiner. Amy and I intend to marry in four weeks. The banns are being read at church this Sunday. The wedding will be small, at my family's church in Greens Norton."

It took Will a moment to process what Nick was saying. Not that he intended to marry Amy, that was no surprise. But that Nick Greene was a Greene from Greens Norton. He had no idea his friend came from such nobility.

"Nick Greene from Greens Norton," Will finally said. "I'm impressed."

"Don't be. I'm the youngest son of a long line of youngest sons. I have the name, and that's about it."

"Still, will your family accept Amy? She is not of noble blood."

Nick stopped. "Will, look at me. I am a pock-marked man who has little chance of inheriting anything. My name got me the job with Gardiner, but that's where my influence ends. My parents are happy I found someone I love. They're relieved I will not end up their aging, unwed child, lurking around taverns, embarrassing them with my drunken antics."

Will slapped Nick on the back. "Very well! I am happy for you, happy for Amy."

"Will you come to the wedding?" Nick asked hopefully. "At St. Bartholomew's in Greens Norton? I know it's a bit of a distance."

"If I can get away from here," Will said. "It's what? A two-day ride?"

"Two days. An easy ride. The weather should be good in late June, and the roads dry."

"Then count on me," Will said. "I'm sure Sir Thomas won't deny my presence at the wedding of my sister and my friend."

Nick smiled. "It will be good of you to come," he said. "Meaningful to both Amy and to me."

When Nick left that evening, Will had plenty to ponder. As Nick indicated, Thomas More had fallen from King Henry's grace, and court positions seemed more tenuous than usual. The only people who seemed secure were Thomas Cromwell and, by extension, Richard Rich.

Will knew he had to make contact with Thomas More. He had been in Chelsea for a month and had uncovered no information whatsoever. He knew he needed something - anything - for Rich, who would, undoubtedly, send Angus to badger him if he waited

THE FAILED APPRENTICE

much longer. And now he needed to ask More for time to travel to Greens Norton. But More was elusive. He remained holed up with his advisors and his family most of the day, and at night he ate quickly and retired to bed at 9:00. A swirl of activity followed him; Will needed to get the man alone.

So one evening, after May had turned to June and Nick and Amy's wedding was only two weeks off, Will watched as Thomas More left his family in the middle of the evening meal. Will stood, excused himself, and followed More out into the gardens. Although More was walking slowly, heading toward his chapel, Will needed to run to catch up. "Sir Thomas," he said when he got closer. He was slightly out of breath. For a moment, Will chided himself for falling out of shape, for getting soft with good food and an easy life.

More turned around. "Ah, it's the tutor Will," More said, smiling. "I was hoping we would meet soon. But, as you undoubtedly know, I've been a little preoccupied."

Will looked at More - he was not a big man, but his shoulders were broad, and his presence formidable. "It's an honor to meet you, Sir Thomas," Will said.

"We shall walk," More said. "I'm heading to my library. Have you seen it?"

"I have not," Will said, falling into step with More.

"Then you are in for a treat." The two men arrived at the smaller brick outbuilding, and More opened the thick oak door.

The library smelled musty, and the evening light illuminated the swirling dust motes floating throughout the room. Books of every size lined the walls, and a small desk stood in the corner. A brass candlestick sat atop the desk; a beeswax candle burned close to the nub in its holder. Papers were strewn haphazardly on the desk's surface, and a quill pen lay to the side, a dollop of ink staining a small piece of fabric on which it rested.

"I like to work here at night, on those evenings when sleep eludes me," More said. "I hate to keep Alice awake. She's quite disagreeable if she doesn't get her rest."

Will laughed. "This is a beautiful library," he said as he slowly dragged his fingers across the leather spines of the volumes closest to him.

"This," More said, pulling out a book, the leather cover worn. "Was written by my friend Desiderius Erasmus. An amazing scholar. *Handbook of a Christian Knight*, it's called. A great story about faith and living as a true Christian. You may borrow it if you like."

More handed the book to Will. The leather was soft, supple. Will opened the book and saw the parchment was thin, almost brittle. The book had been well read. "Thank you," he said. "I will read it and take good care of it."

"Now," More said, sitting in his desk chair and fingering the quill. "You didn't chase me down in the garden in hopes of me loaning you this book. What can I do for you?"

Will cleared his throat and explained about Nick and Amy's marriage and Will's desire to take a week off to travel to Greens Norton.

"I've met Nick Greene; Gardiner thinks highly of him." More nodded his approval. "He's marrying your sister? A good match. Of course, you may have time off." More stood and searched through a row of books. Finally, he pulled another book from his shelf and handed it to Will. "A wedding gift for the couple. Another book by Erasmus, *On Civility in Children*. They may need this soon. I assume your sister can read?"

"Amy is a good reader," Will said proudly, overwhelmed by the two books in his hands.

"Good. Women should be educated," More said. "My daughters are more learned than most men."

"Thank you, Sir Thomas," Will said, smiling. "I know Amy and Nick will cherish such a generous gift."

"I like to see young people happy," More said. "And young people remain in the faith."

Will nodded and looked around but had lost all desire to spy after receiving such gifts. "I best leave you to your work," he said as he turned to leave.

THE FAILED APPRENTICE

As Will walked back to the house, the leather of the books warmed his hands, and he smiled. But then he remembered Rich's words, that More could be kind, charming. That life in Chelsea could be agreeable, soft. Once again, Rich was right.

Chapter 18

Two weeks later, Will rose early to prepare for the trip to Greens Norton. He had instructed Rory to prepare Baucent, with whom he had developed a man/horse detente, for the two-day ride.

Dawn had just broken as Will left the house, bidding Mags, who was scurrying about the kitchen, goodbye. "Safe travels, Will," she said, handing him a sack filled with bread and cheese. She grinned. "For the road."

Will thanked her; in the short time he had been at More's home, he had grown fond of the gentle, older woman. "See you in a week," he said.

Will walked outside and headed toward the stables. The morning was quiet, the air moist with humidity and the ground covered in dew. Will looked at his leather boots as he walked through the grass; the toes were already dark from the moisture. Up ahead, he noticed two additional impressions of shoes in the grass. One large, one small. One male, one female. Will increased his pace, following the footsteps.

Will did not need to go much farther to hear whispered voices from a copse near the stables. He skirted around the low branches of an apple tree and peered around the tree's trunk. Up ahead, he saw Phoebe talking with a man.

Jealousy coursed through Will's veins. So this was why Phoebe was so elusive. This was why she never seemed to seek Will out, return his shy smile, engage him in anything more than the most banal pleasantries. Will admonished himself. What a fool he had been. Of course, she already had a man.

But then Phoebe and the man shifted positions. Will looked closer as Phoebe gestured, and the man, nodding, turned to face Will. It was Angus.

Will watched them, confused. What was Angus doing with Phoebe? Was he courting her? Or was Angus there to see him and had run into Phoebe? Why hadn't Rich let him know Angus was

THE FAILED APPRENTICE

coming? Will leaned against the hard bark of the apple tree, his heart hammering.

Phoebe and Angus continued their animated discussion for several moments. Then, Angus nodded, and they turned, walking toward the house. Will panicked, but as they passed, he remained undetected. "I'll be back in two weeks," he heard Angus say.

Will watched as they parted, and Angus headed toward the stables, where he mounted his horse and rode off. So he was not there to see Will after all. Will watched Phoebe head back to the house.

Will's first instinct was to run after Phoebe, to ask her what Angus wanted with her. He took a few tentative steps back to the house but stopped when he heard anxious whinnying coming from the stables. It sounded like Baucent. He turned to the stables, then back to the house, but Phoebe was already inside. He would deal with this when he returned from Greens Norton.

Baucent was agitated when Will entered the stables, stomping his hooves and snorting. Rory had Baucent by the reins and was trying to calm him; the horse's eyes were wild, haunted, as he attempted to rear back.

"What happened?" Will said as he reached to stroke Baucent's neck.

"He was fine until that man came," Rory said. "That burly cur who was just here. Baucent took one look at him and went wild." Rory offered the horse a carrot, which Baucent refused, twisting his neck and straining at the reins.

Will seethed. Not only was Angus slithering around Phoebe and lurking around More's home, but Will was sure Angus had abused the horse. "Give me the carrot," he said. He continued to stroke Baucent's neck; eventually, the horse calmed and took the offering. "Don't let Baucent near him if he comes back."

Rory nodded. "That man's a right churl," he said. "My brother works in Sir Thomas' gardens. That arse makes a point of tramping over the flowerbeds."

Eventually, Baucent calmed enough for Will to mount him and start the journey northwest to Greens Norton. He felt his coin purse under his cloak, pressing against his ribs. He had brought enough money to find a suitable inn for the night. This time, he would not fall for schemes from men like Fergus.

Greens Norton was a village that dated back to the Middle Ages and was originally royal lands of William the Conqueror. Close to a Roman settlement, the town had grown slowly as the years passed and was ultimately sold to Sir Henry Greene in the 14th century for twenty shillings, roughly the cost of two cows or fifty days of labor for an unskilled tradesman. The town continued to grow and prosper, as did the Greene family, whose name became part of the town's heritage. Two days later, as Will rode into Greens Norton, he was impressed by the clean streets, the shops that lined the main road, the cheerful calls of residents. How different from London, he thought.

Will was staying at the Greenes' home outside the village, a large, moated manor that had seen better days but was still impressive if viewed from a distance. The slate roof reflected the sun, as did the many small, diamond-shaped windowpanes. A short stone bridge led over the moat to a solid oak door with an iron grille at eye level. Will handed Baucent to a stablehand and crossed through a small garden to the home.

Before Will reached the bridge, the door flew open, and Amy ran out. "You're here!" she shouted as she threw her arms around Will. "You came!"

"Of course I did," Will said. "Do you think I would miss this?"

Amy smiled. Gone were the remnants of Culler's abuse. Will pushed the image of Amy, bruised and wan, from his mind. She looked nothing like that shell of a girl, nothing at all.

Will and Amy crossed the bridge and entered the home. A large stone fireplace took up much of one side of the wall in the great hall with the Greene coat of arms painted above it. "Sit," Amy said, motioning to a heavy wooden chair with a plump embroidered cushion. "Let me get you some ale." She disappeared into a back room as Will kneaded his shoulders which were sore despite an easy ride.

THE FAILED APPRENTICE

Moments later, Amy emerged with a tankard of ale for Will. He was parched from the journey and drained the cup quickly.

The siblings caught up - Amy asked about life at More's, about which Will remained elusive. Amy had recently quit work at Winchester Palace to focus on Nick. "I hope we have a baby soon," she said. "I want a family of my own."

"Just remember our parents," Will said. "All those children, what it did to them. Please don't make the same mistake."

A darkness passed over Amy's face, glazing her eyes if only for a moment. "What is it?" Will said.

Amy looked around the room and lowered her voice. "I don't want Nick to know, but I went home," she said.

"You saw our parents?"

"Yes." Amy sighed. "It did not go well." She looked down and picked at her thumbnail. "I wanted to tell them I was to be married, that I was marrying a respectable man. A good man." She hesitated.

"And?" Will asked. "What happened?"

Amy looked up and shook her head. "Father was screaming at John when I arrived. John had done something, gotten himself into some sort of trouble. He was cowering in the corner, and Father was carrying on like a lunatic. I walked in, and he turned his abuse on me. He wouldn't let me get a word out; he called me a common thief. He thought I was there hoping to move back with the family. He told me to get out."

"I can't believe he still thinks you stole from Culler. Does he know what happened to him? That he was hanged for smuggling?"

"I don't know if he knows or not, but he still thinks I stole from him, regardless of Culler's end. Father pushed me out the door and bolted it." Amy's shoulders slumped. "He wouldn't listen to me. I never should have gone back."

Will nodded. "You tried, Amy. Nick is now your family. As am I. And all these Greenes."

"It's just hard, Will. Our parents will have nothing to do with me."

Will looked at Amy and thought of their parents, their slow slide into poverty, their systematic rejection of their children. First Will, then Amy. Will shook his head. "Best try and forget them. Look ahead, Amy. You have so much to be happy about." As if on cue, Nick entered the room, beaming.

"Will, I thought that was you," he said. "I saw you as you rode in. Just in time for the wedding tomorrow!" Nick embraced Will and slapped him on the back.

Over Nick's shoulder, Will nodded at Amy, and an understanding passed between the two. They would be each other's family, as Will said. Aside from Nick, they were all each other had.

The following day Will walked Amy to St. Bartholomew's, the ancient church in Greens Norton that had been the Greenes' church for centuries. Originally a Saxon church, the first building on the site dated back to the 600s, when Greens Norton was called Norton Davey, and the Greenes had yet to occupy this slice of Northamptonshire. The church, at the crest of a hill, was made of stone, with a sharp spire ascending heavenward. The ceremony took place outside, at the church door, which was canopied with flowers. Will watched as Nick and Amy exchanged vows, as the priest blessed the wedding ring, as Nick placed the ring on Amy's finger. As the ceremony continued, he observed the congregants. Nick's family was not large, although his three older brothers' presence was enough to remind Will that Nick would miss out on any inheritance. Yet the family seemed kind; they eagerly embraced Amy. Her modest origins appeared to cast no shadow on their noble lineage.

Once the vows were said, Will followed the group into the church for the marriage mass. The inside was cool and musty, and the ghostly scent of incense still hung in the air. As the priest droned on, his voice low and lulling, Will stopped listening and began to think of his own life. He thought of Philippa, how life with her would have been simple, if unfulfilling. He thought of Phoebe, whose appeal was undeniable but who vexed Will in

THE FAILED APPRENTICE

almost every way. He was a young man, barely twenty. But perhaps he was meant to live this life out alone.

After the mass, the crowd dispersed with plans to meet at the Greenes' home for a celebratory feast. Lingering behind, Will remained in the church, taking in the coolness of the dark wood and ancient Saxon walls. His footsteps echoed on the stone floor as he walked toward the nave. With the church empty of bodies, the mustiness of dust and sweat dissipated; the air felt clean.

A noise startled Will, and he looked up to see a sparrow flying from the ceiling, trapped and panicked. It careened into the stained-glass windows and flew frantically along the walls, searching for an escape. Will watched the bird's erratic path until it found the open door. He exhaled slowly, aware of his pounding heart. You and me both, he thought. If only my situation was as easy as finding an open door.

Will walked down the north aisle. Dead Greenes seemed to be everywhere - tombs, plaques, alabaster effigies. In an alcove, a brass rendering of Sir Thomas Greene and his wife, Matilda Throckmorton, was surrounded by candles. Greene died in 1462, seventy years ago. Will paused, looking for a resemblance to Nick. The brass drawing was rudimentary, lacking in detail. Dead Tom Greene could have been anyone. Will traced the effigy with his fingers, the brass cold to the touch.

"You're admiring my great grandparents?" A soft voice said, causing Will to start. A tall woman walked up behind him, her strawberry blonde hair creeping out of her blue mantle. A kind smile spread across her face. Although she appeared close in age to Will, her dress and demeanor indicated maturity. "Probably not a realistic likeness."

"You must be one of the many Greenes," Will said. "I'm Will Patten. Amy is my sister."

The woman smiled. "There are a lot of us Greene descendants," she said. "Although getting fewer and fewer. I'm afraid our branch will die off if more babies aren't born. Perhaps Amy and Nick can help out there." She laughed a throaty laugh. "I'm Katherine Parr. Nick is my cousin. My mother was a Greene."

"Kate," a man's voice said, followed by a hacking cough that echoed in the empty church. "You best come."

"My husband, Edward Burgh," she said, nodding to the back of the church. "He's not well. I should be going. Nice to meet you, Will." Kate Parr laid a hand on Will's shoulder; her fingers were long and elegant. "Perhaps we shall meet again."

"I look forward to it," Will said, watching Kate Parr's graceful form turn, walk to her husband, and take his arm.

At the wedding feast, Will gave Amy and Nick the book from More, which he had wrapped in muslin given to him by Mags. "I have something for you as well," Nick said and handed Will a small box. "For watching out for Amy. And for being a friend to me."

Will opened the intricately carved box. Inside was the pocket sundial Will had admired months before when he and Nick were just becoming friends. The sundial Stephen Gardiner had given to Nick. "I can't accept this," Will said. "It's from Gardiner. I know how much it means to you."

"You will accept it and stop your mewing," Amy said. "It's from both of us."

"Very well," Will said, smiling. He was overwhelmed. A lump formed in his throat, and his eyes began to glaze with tears. Embarrassed, he turned away.

"Oh, stop," Amy said. "You will make me cry."

Will returned to his chamber that evening after much wine and a startling amount of food. On his bed was a note, Rich's stamp embossed in blood-red sealing wax. Although his head swam, Will tore open the letter and read it. It was a summons from Rich to stop at Whitehall on his way back to Chelsea. A chill passed through Will. It did not matter where Will went; Rich knew his every move.

Will slept poorly that night. Perhaps it was the wine, perhaps it was his upcoming meeting with Rich, but Will tossed and turned and eventually rose before the sun and began his journey back to Chelsea via London. The following afternoon, as Will rode into London and toward Whitehall, Baucent became aggressive. He

THE FAILED APPRENTICE

nipped at horses he passed, strained at his reins, and stomped his hooves on the dusty road, kicking up dirt and stones. Eventually, as they approached Whitehall, he stopped and refused to go further.

Will handed Baucent to a stablehand several streets away from Whitehall with instructions to treat him gently. "I recognize this horse," the stablehand said. "He was a gentle foal until he spent time with that scarred huff Angus." The stablehand patted Baucent's neck. "I'll give him extra care."

Will fumed as he marched toward the palace and Rich's chamber. His suspicions were confirmed; Baucent had suffered under Angus' brutality. Will knocked on Rich's door and then entered, not waiting for an invitation.

"Your man, Angus," Will said through gritted teeth. "He was cruel to my horse. The poor beast could barely get close to Whitehall without bucking me off."

"Well, hello to you too, Will," Rich said. "Sit down and stop your whining."

"You don't care your man is abusing his horses?"

Rich shrugged his shoulders. "Angus," he said. "What do you expect?"

Will threw himself onto a heavy chair; the furnishings in Rich's chamber had improved. The chair cushions were plump and looked new, the weave unworn. Rich, too, appeared to have gained weight and had an even greater air of superiority about him. "What's going on with Angus and Phoebe?" Will asked, picking a piece of mud off the heel of his boot.

"Who?" Rich replied.

"Angus and Phoebe Houghton."

"I don't know who that is," Rich said. "And please stop flicking the mud from your boot on my floor."

Will moved his hand away from his heel. "I don't have much to tell you if that's why I'm here," he said. "More just returned from London and has been holed up with his advisors. I did meet him, though, so there's that."

"Good," Rich said. "Time to step it up, though. It's not enough that he's been removed from court. We need to keep him out of favor with the king. He needs to be wholly discredited. I've known More since I was a boy. Under the right conditions, he can be a gossipmonger."

Will leaned back, his hands kneading the chair's arms. "He hasn't mentioned anything to me about the king," he said. "Or the faith. But he did give me a book on being a good Christian."

"That's a good start," Rich said. "Now increase your efforts. Listen at doors if you have to."

"I'll try," Will said.

"You best do more than *try*." Rich knotted his eyebrows threateningly.

Will and Rich regarded each other for a moment. "Very well," Will said.

"Good. If you find something, send a message to me. Otherwise, Angus will be stopping by in a couple weeks. Unannounced."

Will stood up to leave. "I'll be in touch," he said.

"By the way," Rich said. "Philippa misses you." He guffawed. "She's pining away. I'd hate for anything to happen to her." He made a lewd gesture with his index finger.

Will turned. "You can't be serious," he said. "Leave Philippa out of this."

Rich leaned back, his smile lecherous. He kissed the air and laughed.

"I mean it," Will said. "She is an innocent girl."

"Let's hope she stays that way. Now, get going. More will be waiting," Rich said, smirking.

Will left Whitehall feeling dirty. His clothes were covered in dust and mud from the journey, but he felt his soul was blackened, too. The meeting with Rich had soured the happiness he felt at Amy and Nick's wedding. He worried about Philippa. As Will knew, Rich was capable of anything.

A week passed. Will was anxious to get More alone but had been unsuccessful. More continued to sequester himself,

THE FAILED APPRENTICE

remaining unattainable to Will. Every night Will's anxiety grew, and his sleep was racked with thoughts of the gallows, the filthy cell in the Tower, and a dishonored Philippa.

During this time, Mags told Will she had learned of omens that plagued the country: two gigantic fish had been found dead, floating in the Thames. A horse's head had burst into flames. A blue cross rose in the sky and blocked the moon. "It's the king," she confided in Will. "He's gone against the natural order of things, putting his wife aside like that." She crossed herself. "God help us."

Yet Will was successful in one aspect since his return to Chelsea: he was able to confront Phoebe. The girls finished their lessons and had gone riding with their father, William Roper. Will found Phoebe in the garden, attempting to peer into More's library through a low window.

"Phoebe," Will said, approaching her through the orchard.

Phoebe jumped. "You startled me, Will," she said as she moved away from the window.

"Did you see anything good through the window?"

"Oh, that." Phoebe waved her hand at the window, but panic filled her eyes. "Lizzy left her doll someplace. I thought it might be in the library."

"Right," Will said, not believing her. He paused. "I saw you with that rough churl Angus before I left for Greens Norton. What was he doing here?"

Phoebe coughed and looked around. "I don't know who you mean," she finally uttered, covering her mouth with her hand.

Phoebe was lying, and she knew Will knew she was. Any trepidation Will had felt about talking to her was gone. She was dissembling. They had that in common. "You know who I mean."

Phoebe rallied. Standing taller, she looked Will in the eye. "And how do *you* know Angus?" she asked.

"Ha!" Will laughed and pointed his finger at her. "So you do know that cur. You need to work on your lying."

"I'm a fine liar, thank you," Phoebe replied.

Will hesitated. "Is he your suitor?" he asked.

Phoebe's eyes widened. "Certainly not. He's a horrible man."

"Then…," Will prompted.

Phoebe opened her mouth and closed it in rapid succession. "You look like a fish," Will said.

"I can't really tell you. Let's just say I'm more than a governess."

Will felt a shock move through his body. He stared at her. "Rich?" he finally said.

Phoebe looked at Will with equal shock. She bit her lower lip and finally said, "Cromwell."

Will felt the strength leave his legs. He sat heavily on the ground, a rotting apple pressing into his thigh. "Thomas Cromwell?"

Phoebe sighed. "Yes." Then quickly: "You cannot tell anyone. I would be killed - literally killed - if this came out." She looked at Will, who was staring at her in disbelief. "Wait," she said. "How do you know Angus?"

"Rich," Will said.

Phoebe gathered her skirts and sat beside Will, deftly avoiding the rotten fruit on the ground. "We are working on the same thing?" she asked.

"More?" Will said.

"More."

"Then perhaps we should join forces. That way, we both escape the gallows."

Phoebe nodded. "Or swing together."

"What does Cromwell have on you?" Will asked. "I doubt you'd volunteer for this job."

"Sadly, it did not take much. My parents had both just died. I was alone, taking in washing, trying to survive. Cromwell found me - I was poor, dirty, tired, and hungry. He offered me an easy life in exchange for information." Phoebe balled up her skirts in her fists. "I made a deal with the devil. But I was desperate, you know? I was young, and I was starving. I started out as a servant. I was supposed to pass along information I got from Queen Katherine's ladies-in-waiting. I must have given him what he

THE FAILED APPRENTICE

wanted because he moved me here shortly after." She sighed. "And you? How did Rich get you?"

"I tried to steal from him." Will looked at Phoebe, expecting her to be shocked. Instead, she nodded. "He caught me and gave me a choice. Work for him or die. Because I can read, I was spared. But he always reminds me how close I am to swinging from the rope."

"Well, Will, we are in the same soup together. So we might as well take advantage of it."

Will saw a tear trickle down Phoebe's cheek. "It will be fine," he said. "Don't worry."

"You have no idea how lonely I've been. My parents are dead, I have no siblings, and now I'm yoked to Cromwell. I can't get close to anyone because of the dirty work he has me doing. I live in fear of slipping up. And then the guilt! More has been kind to me, given me a home much nicer than the one I came from." She wiped her face with the back of her hand. "But I have to survive."

Will reached out and took Phoebe's hand. "I understand. I'm in the same situation, Phoebe. My parents will have nothing to do with me; my sister and her new husband are the only family I have. We'll get through this together." He paused. "We will both survive this."

Phoebe nodded and squeezed Will's hand, then released it. "Then we have each other," she said as she stood. "Meet me here tonight, right after the meal. There have been things going on in the chapel. Something that might help us." She wiped her hands on her skirts. "Sometimes I hope I find out something damning, other times I hope I don't."

Will stood up and brushed the rotting apple from his leg. "Tonight," he said. "I'll be here."

Phoebe turned and headed back to the house, leaving Will feeling stunned. So many questions had been answered that afternoon. He hoped his luck was beginning to change.

Chapter 19

That evening Will met Phoebe after the family supper. More left the table abruptly after the first course; this was normal. More usually ate the first thing served and drank a glass of water, then excused himself or huddled with his wife or the Ropers. He rarely ate more than the first course, and Will had seen him drink alcohol only a handful of times.

After the meal, Will slipped away to meet Phoebe. As the sun slid behind the trees, bathing the world in pinks and purples, Will picked his way through the orchard to the chapel. Phoebe was already there, waiting. Normally, Will would consider brazenly spying on More too risky, but now that Phoebe was involved, it felt like a game. He was excited for the first time since Rich sent him to Chelsea.

"Good, you're here," Phoebe whispered, inching closer to Will. He caught the scent of lavender from her soap and noticed her skin looked rosy, creamy, and soft. He resisted the urge to reach out and touch her face. Shadows from the trees disappeared into the folds of her gown, and the fading dappled light played on the whiteness of her neck. He could not stop staring.

"What is the matter with you?" Phoebe asked, forcing Will to refocus his thoughts. "Come on, More is in the chapel."

Will and Phoebe slunk up to the window, which had a direct view into the chapel. A spiderweb clung to the glass, a dead fly caught in the web. Will brushed the filaments away. The web was sticky, filmy; the fly's body hardened into a tiny black pellet. Will wiped his hand on his jerkin; with the web gone, Will's view was unobstructed.

Inside the chapel, More had lit a candle, the light casting long shadows against the stone walls. Will watched as More removed his cloak and doublet, then peeled off his silk shirt. Phoebe's eyes widened. "What's that?" she asked, staring at Will, her eyes huge.

THE FAILED APPRENTICE

More stood in the center of the room, a short, sleeveless undergarment covering his back and chest. Will strained his eyes against the darkness. "It's a hair shirt," he said.

Phoebe looked incredulously at Will. "A hair shirt? What's that?"

"I'll explain later," Will whispered.

Will continued to watch as More removed the hair shirt and laid it on a chair. In the flickering candlelight, the scars on his back seemed to ripple. Some were new, red, and angry. Some were old and fading, blending with his pale skin.

More walked to a small chest, opened it, and removed a thick wooden rod with three leather knots attached to the end. Will sighed. He knew what this was for.

Will watched as More approached the altar and knelt, his lips moving in prayer. Then, More made the sign of the cross, picked up the stick, and proceeded to whip himself. Even through the thick walls, Will could hear the crack and pull of leather on flesh. Phoebe turned away. "I can't watch this," she said.

Will also turned away. Thanks to his brother Osman's religious fervor, Will was acquainted with both the hair shirt and ritualistic self-mortification, although Osman participated in neither.

Will and Phoebe moved far enough away so More's scourging could no longer be heard. "What was that?" Phoebe said, rattled.

"He's inflicting pain upon himself. Some people do it to cleanse their sins. Others do it as a form of devotion." Will shook his head. "The scourge, it's an ancient practice. During the Black Death, groups of these flagellates would go from town to town, whipping themselves, hoping their pain would cause God to show mercy, to end the plague. Obviously, it didn't work."

"And the hair shirt?"

"The hair shirt," Will sighed. "It's a shirt made of goat hair. It's very painful against the skin, especially if you have open wounds. People wear hair shirts as a means of penance. It's modeled after John the Baptist's shirt, a shirt made of camel hair. Thomas Becket was wearing one when he was martyred."

"How do you know this?" Phoebe said, gaping at Will. "Are you…," she motioned to his upper body.

"Good Lord, no," Will said, involuntarily bringing his hands to his chest. "My brother Osman was extraordinarily religious. He loved to talk about hair shirts and such, although he liked the creature comforts too much to ever wear one." Will paused, then laughed. "He would be angry if his bedding was soiled. He's a monk now."

Phoebe bit her lip. "I never heard of such things."

Will put his hand on Phoebe's back and led her away from the chapel. "It's a different mindset, one I don't understand," Will said. "Even as a small boy, Osman saw things differently than the rest of the family. While I was playing with wooden swords, Osman toddled around the house, clinging to a crucifix he made from sticks. As he got older, he would fast, but I thought that was because he didn't like my mother's cooking. He made his own prayer beads from dried beans. My parents wanted him to follow my father, to be a draper. But he refused. He wore them down until they let him enter the monastery. He left when I was working at Topside's."

Phoebe considered this for a moment. "My family went to church, to mass. My parents were good Catholics. But I don't understand wearing a hair shirt or beating yourself. Perhaps your experience with your brother can help you with More."

Will sighed. "I don't know. Even Osman remains a mystery to me."

By now, the sun had set, and the full moon rose over the treetops, impossibly large and deep orange. "The moon," Phoebe said. "It's huge."

The moon seemed so close that Will could touch it. It cast a long swath on the orchards, the gardens, and the imposing walls of More's home. Will turned to Phoebe. "The moon," he said. "It's lit up your face."

Phoebe returned Will's gaze. "There are moonbeams in your eyes."

THE FAILED APPRENTICE

Will touched Phoebe's face and brushed her cheek with his index finger. Her lips parted in response.

"What does it mean?" Phoebe said, her breath soft as air. "The moon is shining as bright as the sun. Is this a good omen for us?"

Will's thumb gently traced her lower lip. "How could it not be?" he said, gently taking Phoebe in his arms. When he kissed her, thoughts of Rich, More, Angus, and Cromwell fled from his mind. All he could think of was the woman in his arms, the softness of her lips, the curve of her waist, the firmness of her back against his palms. The brutality of More's self-flagellation seemed incomprehensible while holding this woman to whom he was so drawn.

Phoebe finally pulled away from Will. "Is this a good idea? I mean, we're both here to do a job. We have Angus breathing down our necks. I don't want to compromise you, or me for that matter."

Will smiled. "Let's allow ourselves this," he said. "Forget Angus, forget Cromwell. We'll do what is expected, but we deserve some happiness, too."

Phoebe smiled. "Then we must be careful," she said. She ran her hand down Will's arm, her touch sending sparks through the rough cotton of his shirt.

"We will be," he said as he leaned in for another kiss.

Phoebe put her hands on his chest. "I best be getting back to the girls," she said. "Remember, we have to be careful." Although there was a warning in her voice, she smiled.

"Yes, careful," Will said, sighing. He turned and followed Phoebe into the house.

As he stretched out on his bed that night, Will smiled. A warm breeze blew in through his window, the sheets cool against his skin, the moon casting a golden beam across Will's bed. Will felt warmth spread through his body, a sense of peace he hadn't felt in so long. He was in a beautiful home; he was well-fed and clothed. Amy was settled with Nick, and he had met a woman who understood him and the strange situation in which they found themselves. He would report More's self-abuse to Angus; perhaps this detail - which Will viewed as relatively insignificant - would get Rich off his back for a while. Then he could concentrate on Phoebe and finding some happiness on the twisting path of his life.

THE FAILED APPRENTICE

Chapter 20

The summer of 1532 ended, and autumn progressed much the same. Will and Phoebe met almost nightly in secret - in the orchard, behind the stables, by the Thames - their assignations growing in longing but also binding them in friendship. Both reported More's behavior to Angus separately, and nothing seemed to come from it. They breathed easier. Many afternoons that autumn, Will took Baucent on rides through More's property or along the Thames. On one such afternoon, Will turned Baucent down a path along the river, away from London and toward the countryside. Birch leaves fell from trees like coins - golds, reds, and yellows, swirling around Will and cracking under Baucent's hooves. Will had little on his mind - a new lesson for the Roper girls, his next meeting with Phoebe, when he could steal away for a few days to see Nick and Amy, who had settled in a small house in Billingsgate across the river from Southwark. Not long into the ride, he heard hoofbeats behind him, overtaking him. He pulled Baucent's reins and directed him to the side of the path. Slowing Baucent to a walk, Will waited for the other rider to pass.

Yet the rider did not pass but pulled up alongside Will. The horse was a dapple gray jennet, its gait smooth, its muscles toned and strong. It was More's favorite horse.

Will looked to the rider and was surprised to see More in the saddle. "Sir Thomas," Will said, bowing his head as Baucent dipped his as well.

"You've done a good job training your horse to bow," More said, laughing.

"He knows his place," Will also responded with a laugh.

"Smart horse," More replied. "There are many at court who think that is a lesson I should learn. Maybe your horse can teach me."

"I'm not sure Baucent is much of an instructor," Will said. "He struggles with the English language."

"Don't we all?" More said. Will laughed. More's gift as a writer and speaker was legendary.

The two rode in silence for a while, the only sound being the Thames lapping the shore and leaves crunching under the horses' hooves.

"Do you know what's going on in court?" More said, breaking the silence. "Perhaps your friend Nick Greene has kept you updated?"

"I haven't seen Nick since his wedding to my sister," Will replied. "I know pretty much nothing that's going on in London."

"It must be nice to not care about the machinations of government. I still seem to have one foot stuck in Westminster when all I want is to be left alone in Chelsea. Count yourself fortunate."

If you only knew, Will thought. But then he realized this was an ideal scenario: he had More alone and More seemed relaxed around him. Perhaps he could get More to talk, to divulge something he could relay to Rich, who had recently sent Angus to Chelsea to demand more information.

Will cleared his throat. "What's vexing you, Sir? I can't imagine things could be that bad."

More hesitated. "I think you should go to London for a couple days and spend time with Greene and your sister. I understand Gardiner is even more out of favor than before - almost as out of favor as I am. The king recently appointed Thomas Cranmer as the new Archbishop of Canterbury. He passed over all the English bishops, including Gardiner, in favor of Cranmer. The post should have been Gardiner's. Instead, it has fallen to a Protestant. A Protestant! And rumor has it Cranmer is married - his second marriage at that!"

Will was taken aback. Not only by More's offer for Will to visit Amy and Nick but by the news of the change in church politics. "That is unsettling," he said. "I'm sure Nick is concerned. I would be happy to take leave for a few days."

THE FAILED APPRENTICE

"Margaret and her family are heading to their house in Kent next week for a month. So you may visit your family then."

Will nodded. "I'll plan on that, Sir Thomas," he said. He had been aware of this plan; Phoebe had told him the night before she would be leaving with the Ropers.

"Good. And then you and I can spend some time in my library. I have a couple more books to recommend. Good books on religion."

"I'd enjoy that."

More sighed. "Cranmer won't be consecrated until next year, so there is a glimmer. But the way the court is headed, I hold out very little hope. I understand the king has gone to France with Anne Boleyn to meet with King Francis. He hopes to gain support for the annulment. To appeal to the King of France…," More shook his head as his voice faded away.

Will had no idea how to respond. This was news to him but was surely not to Rich or Cromwell.

"Will," More said, his voice gaining force. "I know you are a Catholic. Promise me you'll adhere to the faith. Things may get complicated for us, those of us who practice the true religion. Don't be swayed by the changing winds moving through the country. Heresy is everywhere," his eyes flashed, and Will was again reminded of the man sitting on the dais as men met their death on the pyre. "I tried to root it out, and I'll try again, but the devil is cunning. He knows many ways to tempt us. He seems to have the king in his grasp. Promise me you will stay loyal to Pope Clement and the Church."

"Of course, Sir Thomas," Will replied. He looked at More, who seemed older, lesser. Will wondered if he was wearing his hair shirt.

As if reading his mind, More continued. "I am not a young man, and I've been feeling the scourge of age. I have a sense that I am not much longer in this world. Sometimes at night, I hear the grave calling me. I don't want to meet the Lord leaving England as it is, faithless, floundering."

"I am sure you have a long life left," Will said. "I'm sure the king will come back to his faith."

More laughed, resigned. "You are an innocent, Will. I wish I could go back to that state again. Back when I was a boy on Milk Street. Sadly, I have seen too much in my many years."

The men continued their ride as dark clouds moved across the sky, blocking the autumnal sun. Will glanced at More, who seemed lost in thought. Finally, More said, "I am done with my ride; it has tired me. Enjoy the day and your fine horse." He turned his jennet and headed back to his home, the sleek horse kicking up dust, hiding his rider in a swirling gray cloud.

The following week, Will left for London. Nick and Amy had recently moved into a small house close to Pudding Lane. Although the name *Pudding Lane* evoked thoughts of confections, "pudding" was actually the term for offal from slaughtered cows that was transported down the street and to the river to be loaded onto waste barges. Will hoped his sister's house was far enough away from what was sure to be a disgusting smell, one that contributed to the overall filth of London's streets.

As Will passed Pudding Lane, the russet-stained cobblestones reminded him of the street's origins, and the faint coppery smell of blood hung in the air, but ever so slight - there, but just out of touch. Worse was the stench of manure and rotting entrails of animals, the parts cast off from the slaughterhouse that had failed to make their way to the waste barge. Flies buzzed and rose in small clouds, and Baucent swished his tail to keep the insects from him. Will waved his hand in a vain attempt to dispel the smell and the flies.

Shortly after passing Pudding Lane, Will turned left onto St. Botolph's Lane. Amy and Nick's house sat in the shadow of St. Botolph's Church, a 12th church dedicated to the 7th-century Anglo-Saxon of the same name. The Greenes' house was set back a bit, away from the refuse that gathered in a stone drain running along the curb. Will left Baucent at a nearby stable and approached the house. The oak door was sturdy and the knocker, an iron deer's head holding a ring in its mouth, was a nod to the

THE FAILED APPRENTICE

buck in the Greene coat of arms. The knocker was cold in Will's grip but weighty. He lifted it and let it fall.

Moments later, the door wrenched open, and Amy stood, beaming, on the threshold. Her hair was undone and thick, and her cheeks flushed with excitement. For a moment, he remembered the shadow of the girl she was after Culler's attack, but the memory was fleeting. "Come in," she said, smiling. "Nick is at the palace but will be back soon."

Amy ushered Will into her home. It was a respectable size, similar to the house on Fenn Lane, but with only two occupants, it felt larger. Unlike Will's family home, though, the floor did not tilt, and it was covered in flagstone instead of rushes. A lazy flame licked a small log in the fireplace, occasionally sending a plume of smoke out and into the room. Amy coughed. "That log's damp," she apologized.

Will laughed. "Did you build that fire yourself?"

"I did," Amy said proudly. "I've gotten quite good at fire building!"

Will looked at the flame, struggling to gain traction against the wet log. It was a start.

Will surveyed the front room. Small windows surrounded the room, letting in plenty of light. A pewter platter with bread and cheese and a jug of ale sat at the center of an oak trestle table; the table looked new. "You must be hungry and thirsty," she said, pulling Will toward the table. "I bought this bread this morning from a baker on Pudding Lane." Amy walked to the table and inched the platter toward Will.

Amy was proud of her efforts to make Will feel welcome - the fire, the food, and the drink. He smiled and tore off the heel of the bread; it was still warm and satisfyingly yeasty and salty.

Looking around, Will saw the house was in the unkempt state he had come to expect from Amy. Dust gathered in the corners, and cobwebs clung to the window frames. But there was also an unmistakable warmth to the room. Nick's doublet casually thrown over the back of a chair, Amy's slippers wedged under a table, an open sideboard filled with white and blue porcelain plates. "You have made this a home," he said.

Nick arrived shortly, followed by an older woman in a stained apron carrying a large, black pot. Once Nick greeted Will, he introduced the woman as Mistress Chapman, who curtseyed to Will. "It's a pleasure, Will," she said, smiling, her wrinkles deep and resembling the skin on a shriveled apple. "I cook for Amy. I clean too. I help out when I can."

"She's blind in one eye," Nick whispered to Will. "That explains the cleaning."

Amy took the pot from Mistress Chapman, put it on the table, and removed the lid. Immediately the room filled with the earthy smell of cloves and cinnamon. "It's mawmenny," Mistress Chapman said proudly. "Amy said it was a special day, with you visiting and all."

Amy entreated Mistress Chapman to stay and share the mawmenny, but she was adamant. "Your brother is here, and I won't interrupt this reunion," she said. "Just enjoy the stew."

The scent of the mawmenny filled the room - wine, sugar, chicken, cinnamon, cloves, and mace - as the three sat at the table to eat, Amy ladling the stew into pewter porringers. That evening, the three finished the mawmenny and a few tankards of ale. Will was sated, and as he and Nick sat by the fire, he felt his eyelids become heavy.

Yet Nick was excited to share news with Will: he would be traveling to Eltham Palace in Greenwich the following day, as the king had just returned from Calais and would be holding court there. Stephen Gardiner would meet join him at Eltham. Would Will like to accompany him? Will did not need to be asked twice; the opportunity to see the moated manor of Eltham was a dream.

Eltham Palace was originally the property of Anthony Bek, the 14th-century Bishop of Durham. He gifted the palace to King Edward II in 1305, and Eltham was the home where a young Henry VIII spent much of his time. Thomas More also visited the palace with his friend, Desiderius Erasmus. More had spoken

THE FAILED APPRENTICE

fondly of his visits to Eltham; now, Will would see the palace first-hand.

The following morning, Will dressed in his most impressive finery, which was not very fine at all. Nick ended up lending him a doublet with slashed sleeves and a plumed hat, elevating Will's appearance substantially. They left for the one-hour ride at first light. Crossing London Bridge, Will resisted turning right to check on Ellyn. Instead, they headed left, rode parallel to the Thames, and turned south halfway into their journey.

Once outside of the congestion of London, Will and Nick slowed their pace. "How's Ellyn?" Will asked. "Are you still collecting money at the Axe?" Will had to admit he missed his old boss, her rough ways, her maternal care for her girls.

"Ellyn?" Nick said, laughing. "That old crone is thriving. Your friend Rich has sent some of his cullies there, and they pay well. I dare say she misses you, though. And the steps are in bad shape again."

Will smiled. He was glad that Ellyn was doing well. He would never forget how she had cared for Amy after Culler's attack. He owed her his loyalty.

"But Ivy," Nick continued. "That's another story. She fell pregnant. An apothecary gave her some concoction, something to get rid of the baby." Nick sighed. "She spent a week in agony after dispelling the child. She did not survive. They buried her at Cross Bones."

Will shook his head. Cross Bones was an unconsecrated burial ground for prostitutes in Southwark. "Poor girl. She didn't even get a proper burial," he said.

Nick shrugged his shoulders, and they rode on in silence, Will unsure if Nick approved of Ivy's shoddy burial or not. Finally, Will broke the silence. "Amy seems happy," he ventured. "She seems quite settled into married life."

Nick smiled. "She is," he said. "I still can't get over my good fortune." Nick lowered his voice, although no one else was around. "But we haven't conceived yet. She is afraid Culler damaged her when he... he...," Nick could not continue.

"Give it time," Will said. That was about all the advice he could, or would want to, give.

"I am happy with it being just the two of us. But Amy, she wants a baby."

Will nodded and breathed a sigh of relief when the towers of Eltham came into view. He was happy to put an end to that conversation.

THE FAILED APPRENTICE

Chapter 21

Eltham Palace sat on the grounds of a manor dating to Saxon times, although there were several incarnations of the palace between then and when it first came into Will's view. A park of nearly 1300 acres surrounded the castle and was a favorite hunting ground for royals and their guests. A tiltyard had been recently constructed east of the moat, and new apartments were being built on the western side. The palace itself was tall and sprawling, made of stone and brick. Will and Nick crossed the wide stone bridge that spanned the moat to the palace's barbican and entered the inner bailey.

Will had been overwhelmed at Winchester Palace's grandeur, but it was nothing compared to the great hall at Eltham. Built during the reign of Edward IV, the hall was cavernous with a soaring oak roof of magnificent hammer beam construction. Light cascaded in through the glazed windows above the gallery, illuminating the ornately tiled floor. Heavy tapestries woven with gold and silver thread lined the walls. The room sparkled.

At least a hundred people were milling about as Will and Nick moved through the hall. Nick seemed to know where he was going, and Will followed a pace behind, staring at those who were surely important members of the king's court. Nick stopped abruptly in front of a tall man who seemed to be entering middle age; slight wrinkles appeared on his forehead and at the corners of his eyes. "Greene," the man said and clapped Nick on the back.

"My Lord," Nick said, beaming. "This is my brother-in-law, Will Patten."

Will had seen Stephen Gardiner before; he occasionally visited Thomas More, although Will had only seen him from a distance. Gardiner was dressed in bishop's robes, his dark hair peeking out of his amaranth biretta. His eyes were sad, Will thought. Such sad eyes on such a prominent man. "Your Excellency," Will said.

Gardiner smiled. "Will Patten," he said. "You work for Sir Thomas, do you not?"

"I do," Will replied. "I tutor Sir Thomas' grandchildren, Margaret Roper's daughters."

"More thinks highly of you," Gardiner continued. "He says you are a smart and inquisitive young man. A devout man."

"Thank you," Thomas replied, a mixture of pride and guilt forming a knot in his stomach.

Gardiner turned to Nick. "Come with me," he said. Then to Will: "Have some nourishment. The food here is excellent." Gardiner turned, and he and Nick disappeared into the crowd.

A long table had been set up at the side of the hall, full of food and drink. Will walked over to the table and picked up a pear. As he lifted it to his mouth, he felt a presence move next to him. "Don't look at me," he heard. Will lowered the pear. He knew the voice.

"Master Rich."

"What are you doing here?" Rich asked, his voice a gravelly whisper.

Will's eyes were affixed to his pear. "I'm here with my brother-in-law."

"Greene, Gardiner's man," Rich said, then laughed. "Tell him not to get too comfortable." Will looked questioningly at Rich. "I said, don't look at me, you little cur. No one should see we know each other."

Will gulped. "What do you mean, comfortable?" Will returned his gaze to the pear.

"Just that. I've said enough. Except that I expect you to start to report back more frequently and with better information."

"I'm gaining More's confidence," Will said.

"I want more information than the man wears a hair shirt. Get to it." Rich grabbed a slice of warm manchet and dipped the bread in a bowl of preserves. He turned and walked away.

Will took his pear and a handful of sugared almonds and leaned against the wall, his back to a tapestry that reached close to the ceiling. Several minutes later, a swarm of people scurried to the front of the room and began congregating around a tall man, his red hair and handsome face hovering several inches above most men's heads. Will inched closer and elbowed past a few men who, like him, were craning their necks to get a better view. "Who is that?" Will asked one of them.

"It's the king, you fool," the man replied.

Will had never seen King Henry and had only heard stories of the king's good looks, charm, and athleticism. He pushed past a few more people and, being tall himself, was able to get a better look.

Stephen Gardiner and several other clerics and courtiers stood next to the king, who was, indeed, strikingly handsome. Tall and broad-shouldered, the king had a golden beard that complemented the gold in his doublet and cloak. He stooped and whispered something to a dark-haired man Will recognized as Thomas Cromwell. Both men began laughing. Moments later, the group, including Gardiner and Rich, walked out of the room, shutting a heavy, iron-studded door behind them. The crowd began to disperse, most heading to the food table.

Will looked around for Nick; surely he wouldn't be with the king? But as Will wandered around the room and then the grounds, Nick was nowhere to be seen. Minutes turned to hours, and although the palace was grand and the grounds extensive, Will eventually grew bored. The sun was already well past the noon mark; Will brought out his pocket sundial and saw that it was close to 3:00.

Moments later, Nick emerged from the palace. "There you are," he said. "Let's go. Amy will be worrying."

Will and Nick fetched their horses and started the journey back to London. As soon as they were away from Eltham, Nick turned to Will. "I met King Henry," he said. "I can't believe it."

"I saw him from a distance," Will said. "What's he like?"

"He's everything I thought he'd be," Nick gushed. "He's smart, funny. Incredibly athletic. Commanding. The kind of king England should have." Nick beamed, then lowered his voice. "He secretly married Anne Boleyn while in France. No one knows.

Just his counselors. And you and me. That was the only way he could get her into his bed."

"But what of Queen Katherine? The king is already married. This can't be right."

"But it *is* right," Nick said. "He's the *king*! And he no longer considers himself married to Katherine. Do you want to be the man to tell him he's a bigamist?"

Will felt uneasy. Although not terribly religious, even he knew this was against church doctrine and natural law.

"He's been to Greens Norton," Nick continued. "He met my parents! We talked about the village and the church. The king, Will. He spoke with me!"

Will opened his mouth to speak, but Nick was so consumed with meeting the king that he kept talking. "Rich was there. Did you see him?"

"I didn't," Will lied. Suddenly everything around him felt sullied and underhanded - his spying on More, the king's alleged secret marriage, even Nick's enthusiasm about the machinations at court.

"He's a prick," Nick continued, his voice loud. "Cromwell's lackey. But he's not dangerous."

How little you know, Will thought. He's probably more dangerous than you can imagine.

Nick continued to rhapsodize about his meeting with the king all the way back to St. Botolph's Lane; about half an hour in, Will tuned out Nick's voice and began to worry about More and the information he needed to uncover and pass on. So Will was relieved to arrive back in Chelsea two days later. It had been good to see Amy and Nick. Will was happy that Amy was settled, content in her marriage, in love with his best friend. But Nick's flirting with court politics made Will feel uneasy. Rich's cryptic message about Gardiner worried him. He was sure Nick had no idea what he was getting into and if Gardiner would survive the unrest at court.

Shortly after Will returned, Chelsea was hit with a violent storm. Dark clouds rolled in, the temperature dropped, and the

THE FAILED APPRENTICE

few remaining leaves were stripped from trees and hurled by an angry wind down the corridors of the orchard. Will watched the tempest from the window of More's great hall, the rain's streaks distorting his view, blurring the world around him. He heard a dry cough and turned around; More had quietly entered and was lingering next to a sideboard, touching a large gold bowl, the candlelight from the room reflecting on the brilliant surface.

"Sir Thomas," Will said. "I'm sorry. I didn't see you there."

More looked up. "Will," he said. "This bowl?" He picked up the bowl and held it toward Will. "It was given to me by the king. In better days."

"It's beautiful," Will said. The bowl must have cost a fortune, not that this was something the king, nor More, would need to consider.

More sighed and replaced the bowl on a side table. "I'm worried about the Ropers in Kent. This terrible storm is blowing in from the east. God's wrath. He is displeased." Will felt his stomach clench. If the Ropers were in danger, so was Phoebe. More walked over to the virginal in the corner, the one that Alice More still struggled to play. He tapped out a few notes with his index finger; they sounded hollow. More turned back to Will. "Your friend, Greene - has he heard anything? Anything about Gardiner, court?"

"Nothing, Sir Thomas. He is busy with Bishop Gardiner and keeping my sister happy."

"Gardiner should be cautious. Cromwell has him in his sights," More said. "Amongst others." He pointed to himself. "Just be sure Greene treads carefully. He should keep his opinions close to the vest."

"I'll let him know."

More crossed the room and stood by Will. Both stared at the rain crashing against the glass, tiny arrows trying to get in. "That tree," More pointed to a tall, ancient oak that stood deep in the garden. "I tied heretics to it, whipped them."

Will looked at More, stunned by the revelation. Perhaps he had regret?

"I thought if I could beat them hard enough, long enough, they'd see what a dark path they were on. My lashes were nothing compared to what they'd feel in Hell. Little good it did." He shook his head. "I don't understand it."

So no regret, Will thought.

More paused. "I heard the king has married Boleyn in secret. That's bigamy, Will. A sin. A grave sin."

Will nodded. "Indeed."

"Our country is falling into dark times. This storm is a warning. I fear we may see more of this cosmic unrest."

Will focused on the window, the rain, the trees bending in the wind.

"Well, enough of this," More said, patting Will on the shoulder. "I'll work on getting a message to the Ropers. I won't rest easy until I know Margaret is safe."

Will watched as More left the room, his gait slow, his posture hunched. Will turned and watched the rain; it had not let up. The sky seemed darker, the rain more fierce.

THE FAILED APPRENTICE

Chapter 22

It turned out the Ropers were fine; they would be back in Chelsea before Christmas. Will's heart lightened at Phoebe's imminent return. Yet days later, Rory tracked Will down. "You best come," he said. "Baucent is stomping and snorting; he will not be soothed. It's because that arse is back, sneaking around the stables. You best come and calm your horse."

The arse could only be one person - Angus. Will found him skulking around the stables, trying to peer inside. "Get away from my horse," Will said as he pulled Angus from the stables and toward the orchard.

"Let me go, you churl," Angus said, wrenching his arm out of Will's grip. "I'm here for information. Master Rich is getting fed up with you. And you don't want Master Rich angry."

Will racked his brain. He had little he was willing to give to Angus - More's admission of beating heretics, which was common knowledge. More's seemingly depressed state of mind. Will wanted to keep some things to himself, some things secret. He hemmed and hawed for a bit. "Get on with it," Angus seethed. Then: "I was admiring your sister's house just the other day. Such a cozy place and so close to the churchyard at St. Botolph's. I noticed some new graves being dug over at St. B.'s. The soil was particularly spongy as if waiting for more bodies."

Thomas looked at Angus, incredulous.

"Of course, your sister is quite pretty. Maybe I could have a little fun with her before her visit to the churchyard," Angus continued, smugness darkening his face, his eyes cold.

Will pulled his arm back and threw a punch, aiming at Angus' head. But Angus, if not taller, was much stronger than Will. He grabbed Will's wrist and twisted it, causing Will to crumple. "Hit a nerve, did I?" Angus said, laughing.

"Leave my sister out of this. She has nothing to do with me." Will said, wresting his hand from Angus' grip.

"Your choice, *Master* Patten. Just how much do you love your sister?"

"Fine," Will said, glowering at Angus. "More told me he was concerned about Gardiner, about Cromwell's interest in him. He knows what's going on at court, somehow." Will took a step back. Angus glared at him; clearly, this was not enough. Will sighed. "And he knows about the king's secret marriage to Anne Boleyn. That's all I have and, so help me God, if you lay even a finger on Amy...."

"Yeah, yeah. Amy, Amy." Angus rolled his eyes. "Just keep the information coming, and she'll be fine."

Will watched as Angus sauntered away, pompous, arrogant. At least he kept More's pronouncement of England falling into sin to himself. There was that. But each time Angus showed up, Will was forced to reveal more. It was just a matter of time before Will had to part with information that could be truly damning to More.

Angus' visit sent Will into a spiral of despair. With the Roper girls still in Kent, he had little with which to occupy his time. Most nights, sleep eluded him; most days, he could not eat. As the weather had turned colder, Will spent more time indoors, cloistered in his room, guilt gnawing away at him.

One morning Will awoke after a fitful sleep, a *white night* his mother used to call an evening of tossing and turning. He stretched; his muscles were sore from inactivity and lack of nourishment. Will sat on his bed and looked out his small window. The sun was just starting its ascent, and the ground was covered in frost, sparking and glassy. In the distance, More's chapel glistened in the hoarfrost.

Almost mechanically, Will got up from his bed and donned his warmest wool clothing and a heavy cape. He pulled on his leather boots, now worn and soon to be replaced, and climbed down the stairs to the kitchen. "Will," Mags said, her hand flying to her throat. "You startled me! It's just barely light out. What are you doing up?"

Will forced himself to smile. "I thought I'd go for a walk to clear my head."

THE FAILED APPRENTICE

"Ah, you miss Phoebe. She will be back soon. Just a few days, from what I hear."

Will's eyes grew wide. "Phoebe? But how…."

Mags laughed. "The worst kept secret here," she said, laughing. "You two moon around, staring at each other, sneaking off. You're fooling no one." She sighed. "Young love. How I miss it."

Mags reached into a basket on the counter. "You best put some meat on your bones," she said, handing Will a hot roll. "Fresh from the oven. When Phoebe returns, she won't want to kiss a scarecrow."

Will felt the color creep into his face. He took the bread; it was warm and strangely comforting. "Thank you, Mags," he stammered.

Mags looked at him and laughed.

Will took the roll and fled from the kitchen and out the door which led to the gardens, orchard, and chapel. They had been so careful, he thought. Clearly, not careful enough.

Will managed to eat part of the roll as his boots crunched across the frosty ground. The trees, now bare of leaves, swayed skeletally in the breeze, which, although not strong, was biting. As he neared More's chapel, the bread cooled and felt dry in his mouth. He threw the remains of it into the brush; it would be a fine meal for a squirrel or raccoon.

The door to the chapel was heavy, and Will, tired, weakened, put his shoulder to the frame to open it. He had never been in the chapel without More but felt confident More would not begrudge him this conversation with God.

The chapel was empty and dark, with the faintest hint of sunrise creeping in through the four-centered arched windows that lined the nave. Will approached the chancel, his fingers tracing the cold stone pillars that merged into a pointed arch. The stone was mined from the godstone quarry in nearby Surrey and painted by renowned artist Hans Holbein. Depicted onto the pillars were items that defined More: More's coat of arms; a sword, mace, and scepter; candlesticks and tapers; a missal with ornate clasps; a vial of holy water.

Will entered the chancel and knelt on a small rug in front of the altar. Looking up at the gold crucifix, he breathed deeply. Damn George Topside's soul, he thought. My life was much easier as a blacksmith's apprentice.

The rising sun streamed through the easternmost window, casting light on the crucifix, making it gleam, dust motes swirling in the gold's reflection. A knot formed in Will's gut. What a mess his life was. Amy and Nick were in danger, thanks to him. The gut-searing sense of betrayal and guilt whenever he fed Angus a tidbit of information was eroding his soul. And now Phoebe. They had been so careful, he thought. Perhaps their relationship thrust her in harm's way as well. He thought of his parents and his siblings. How he longed to return to the house on Fenn Road and start all over. Extract joy from running about with a play sword or kicking a ball with Osman.

How do I come back from this, Will wondered. How do I retrieve a vestige of my soul, the parts I haven't given away or corrupted? He looked to his left, eyeing the small chest where More kept his scourge. Maybe there was something to self-mortification. Perhaps the pain on his flesh would drive away the pain in his soul.

Will rejected the idea of the scourge but remembered something Osman had once said. To prostrate oneself in front of God was the ultimate form of surrender, of submission. Will laid his hands on the stone in front of the altar, then lay down completely. The stone was cold against his face, but it felt comforting. He breathed deeply, smelling the echoes of the incense More burned and the earthly timelessness of the godstone. So be it, Will thought. I've messed up enough on my own. Perhaps I need to turn myself over to the something greater.

Will became aware of a hand shaking his shoulder, pulling him roughly out of a dreamless sleep. His face felt almost frozen to the stone; he had drooled while asleep and, leaning back, wiped his mouth with his fingers. "Will, my good Lord, what are you doing?" It was Alice More.

THE FAILED APPRENTICE

The numbing coldness of the stone had stiffened Will's limbs, and he had trouble pulling himself to a standing position. "I must have fallen asleep," he said. "I'm sorry. I didn't mean to intrude on your family chapel," he felt his voice catch. "I didn't know what else to do."

Alice More wrapped her arms around Will, and he folded into her ample body. He buried his face in the fur of her cloak. "You poor man," she said. "What is it? Thomas can be difficult, and I know he's been unloading on you. Sometimes he can't see beyond himself."

Will shook his head. "What time is it?" he asked, noticing the sun was nowhere near where it had been when he had entered the chapel.

"It's near 2:00," Alice said. "How long have you been in here?"

Will was horrified. He had been sleeping on the altar for close to seven hours. "I don't know," Will replied, pulling back from Alice's embrace.

Alice looked at Will and sighed. "The Ropers are back," she finally said. "And your girl Phoebe. I suggest you wash up and change your clothes." She looked at the drool on his cloak and smiled. "I've learned from life with Thomas that things are never easy," she said. "Whatever is bothering you, it will pass." She reached over and squeezed Will's arm.

"I've made some bad choices," he croaked, unaware he was speaking until the words were out.

Alice nodded. "Haven't we all. It's called being human." She put her hand on Will's back and gently pushed him forward. "Now come along, Will. Enough of this. You have a young lady pretending she isn't excited to see you."

Will smiled in spite of himself. "Mags says my relationship with Phoebe is the worst kept secret here," he said.

"There are many secrets here," Alice said. "But I would have to agree. You and Phoebe are the worst kept secret of them all."

That evening Will met Phoebe in their favorite spot in the orchard. Although snowflakes swirled in the air, seeing Phoebe warmed Will. "I snuck out. I think I was undetected," Phoebe said as she wrapped Will in an embrace, her breath coming out in little bursts of mist, her hands seeking warmth under Will's cloak.

"They know, Phoebe. About us. We don't have to skulk around anymore."

Phoebe looked at Will. "Who knows?" she asked. "We've been so careful."

"They all know. Mags knows, which means the whole staff knows. The Mores, everyone. Obviously, we weren't careful enough."

"Well, so be it," Phoebe said, sighing and searching Will's face. "It would come out sooner or later."

Will pulled her back into an embrace; he had missed her, the smell of lavender in her hair, the softness of her skin. "I just want to keep us safe."

"We will be safe," Phoebe said. "No one knows about our connections to Rich and Cromwell."

"Angus has been around, threatening me, threatening Amy and Nick. I don't think I can do this much longer."

Phoebe stepped back and looked Will in the eye. In her, he noticed a resolve he hadn't seen before. "You and I will do what needs to be done," she said. "Regardless. We need to survive this, Will. Then we can get on with our lives." She paused. "Our lives *together*."

Will smiled. "I'll do whatever it takes to make that happen." He held her, kissed her. "I have missed you," he whispered into her ear.

"I've missed you too," Phoebe said, returning his kiss. She pressed herself against Will as he walked her backward until she was tight against a tree; the very tree, Will realized, that More had tied heretics to and beaten. Pushing the thought from his mind, he kissed her as she ran her hands down his back and pulled his hips toward her. Before he knew what he was doing, Will's hand was up Phoebe's skirts while his other hand caressed her breasts. Her thighs were soft and warm, and Will's hand continued up her leg as Phoebe responded with a soft moan. Will removed his other hand from Phoebe's breast and began to pull his breeches down.

THE FAILED APPRENTICE

"Will, stop," Phoebe said, her breath catching. "We can't. I can't risk this."

Will waited a moment, his hand lingering on Phoebe's thigh. "I'm sorry," she said again, her breath hot and airy, and Will pulled back; Phoebe's skirts dropped. She closed her eyes. "I want to," she said, her breath leaving her body in a long exhale. "I am desperate for you. But what if I fall pregnant? It's too great a risk."

"If that happens, then I will marry you, Phoebe," Will said, moving back toward her and taking her face in his hands.

Phoebe kissed his palm. "If we wed, I don't want it to be because I am carrying your child."

Will nodded; Phoebe was right.

"If it makes any difference, I love you," Phoebe said.

Will smiled. "I love you too." Although the words only added to his longing, they at least were a salve to his soul.

Chapter 23

A burden was lifted from Will's shoulders now that his relationship with Phoebe was out in the open; he hadn't thought that sneaking around would be as taxing as it was. Although the Mores welcomed them to stay for Christmas, Will and Phoebe decided a simpler holiday at Nick and Amy's would be more meaningful. Will was anxious to introduce Phoebe to his family.

Will and Phoebe left early Christmas morning, Will on Baucent, and Phoebe on Liard, one of More's gentle gray palfreys. The ride to St. Botolph's Lane was easy, and the pair ambled through the newly fallen snow, following the Thames into London. They rode next to each other and held hands, Will moving Baucent to the forefront when the path narrowed or they came upon other riders. But Christmas morning was not a time when many people were out, and Will and Phoebe cut their own path through the white snow covering the dirt, then cobblestone, roads.

Amy had done her best to decorate their house and beamed with pride as she ushered Will and Phoebe inside. Holly and mistletoe draped the doorframes and mantle, and a yule log - a large log covered in ribbons - was laid in the hearth. A wooden bowl of wassail sat on the sideboard, filling the room with the scents of sugar, apples, and spices.

Once inside, Amy wrapped Phoebe in a hug and kissed her cheek. Phoebe looked at Will with wide eyes, and Amy noticed the slightly panicked look on her face and laughed. "You make my brother happy, so you make me happy," Amy said. "As long as Will's happy, you are family. And I kiss my family."

Phoebe smiled in return and wiped a tear from her eye. To Phoebe, an orphan, Amy's welcome must have felt overwhelming.

"Enough!" Nick said, laughing. "No tears on Christmas Day." He motioned for everyone to sit around the hearth. "We waited for you to light the log, our first as a family." Nick took a lit taper

THE FAILED APPRENTICE

and held it under the log's ribbons, waiting for them to catch. As tradition, the yule log was to burn for the twelve days of Christmas. Will recalled the Mores' yule log - at least five times the size of Amy and Nick's. The Mores would have no trouble keeping that behemoth going for twelve days - Amy and Nick's might last two if they were lucky.

Mistress Chapman appeared shortly after the yule log was lit with a large mince pie - the thirteen ingredients of the pie symbols of Christ and his apostles. Nick implored her to stay, to share the food and wassail. "I'd be honored to join you, as I have no family anymore," Mistress Chapman said matter-of-factly. "They all died during the sweating sickness of 1528." *The same plague that killed my aunt, Topside's wife,* Will thought. He looked at Phoebe, who blanched. That plague had killed her parents as well.

As the group headed toward the table, Amy laughed and pointed at Will and Phoebe. "You're under the kissing bough!" She said. "You best kiss!"

"And make it a good one," Nick said. "Kiss her like you mean it!"

Will looked up and, indeed, was directly under the kissing bough - a wooden hoop interlaced with holly and mistletoe. "Your plan?" teased Phoebe.

Will shrugged his shoulders. "Who am I to go against the kissing bough?" he said as he leaned over and kissed Phoebe, pulling her back in a dip.

"Now that's a kiss," Nick said while Phoebe blushed.

Amy and Nick did their best to create a traditional meal. Starting with plum porridge, the feast was followed by a large platter of sliced brawn in a rich, thick sauce and Mistress Chapman's mince pie. Finally, the wassail, which had cooled but still was aromatic, was served.

Nick filled five wooden tankards with wassail. At the bottom of the bowl, Nick fished out a crust of bread. "For the most important person in the room," he said, laying the sodden slice on a plate. Will smiled at the old tradition; he had received the drenched bread once when he had begun his apprenticeship with Topside.

Nick looked around the room, meeting everyone's eyes. "You are all so important to me," he said. "Mistress Chapman, for caring for Amy and our home. Will, for being a good friend and Amy's protector. Phoebe, for making Will smile more than I have ever seen him smile." Finally, his gaze alighted on Amy, and he laid the bread in front of her. "But my wife," he said, "is the most important person today. I am the luckiest man alive." He paused, looked at Will, and smiled. "And she will be a great mother, too. This summer!"

Amy beamed, and Will stood up and hugged Nick. "A baby," Phoebe said, her eyes sparkling but tinged with wistfulness. "What happy news!" In that moment, when Will saw the longing in Phoebe's eyes, he understood that, above all, she wanted a family. This he could do for her.

After the meal, Will and Nick walked Mistress Chapman back to her home, a large half-timbered home down an alley off St. Botolph's Lane. The older woman had drunk too much wassail and repeatedly stumbled into the street; Nick took her arm and guided her to her front door. "Happy Christmas, Nick, Will," she said as she lurched through her doorway. "I'll be back tomorrow to clean up the mess from today. And stop with the "Mistress Chapman." You best start calling me Lucy."

Nick laughed after Lucy shut her door. "She's almost as good a housekeeper as Amy," he said. "That should tell you all you need to know."

Will and Nick turned back for the short walk home. "Congratulations on the baby," Will said. "Amy must be happy."

"We both are," Nick replied. "We weren't sure it would happen. It took some practice."

Will cleared his throat. He did not want to discuss his sister in this manner. "So," he ventured. "Gardiner. How's it going with him?"

Nick sighed. "He's losing the king's trust. That meeting at Eltham? The king deferred to Cromwell and Cramner. Of course,

THE FAILED APPRENTICE

Gardiner was privy to the king's attention, but Cromwell and Cranmer are favored now. At the expense of Gardiner."

"I have heard that you should be mindful of what's happening at court. Keep your ears open and mouth shut."

"Who told you that?" Nick asked, his eyes growing wide.

"More. Other people of note," Will did not want to mention Rich. "Gardiner seems to be falling from favor. Just watch out. I don't want you cast out with him if that happens."

Nick nodded. "Thank you, but I don't think it will come to that." Nick hesitated, worry creeping into his voice. "Let me know if you hear anything further, though."

As Will and Nick approached the Greenes' door, Will glanced down the lane to St. Botolph's church. Leaning against the church wall, staring in his direction, was a burly man, clearly rough, his posture aggressive. It was Angus. Will could almost see the smirk on his mouth, the scar on his face. Will turned to Nick. "That man, have you seen him before?" Will pointed at the church.

"What man?" Nick said.

Will looked again. Angus was gone.

Will panicked. Why would Angus follow him here on Christmas? Even worse, Angus had seen Phoebe with him.

Shaken, Will entered the house. Phoebe and Amy sat by the hearth, the yule log sputtering, sending errant embers into the room, which quickly died on the flagstone floor. "Phoebe, we best get going," he said.

Amy stood up and looked questioningly at Will. "What's going on?"

"I can't say much," Will said. "Nick, just keep her safe," he motioned to Amy. "Be on the lookout for a big man built like an ape. He has a scar on his face. He's dangerous. Don't engage him. Don't provoke him."

"Angus," Phoebe said, grabbing her cloak. "Oh, dear Lord."

"Who is Angus?" Nick asked.

"He's Rich's henchman. I thought I saw him lurking around here. He meant for me to see him," Will said. "Amy, keep the door bolted. All the time. Don't open it unless you know who is on the other side."

Amy placed a protective hand over her stomach, although it was still flat. "You're scaring me, Will."

"He's not after you," Will said, hoping this was true. "Just be vigilant."

"Will?" Nick asked, looking at Will questioningly.

Will shook his head. "Just be safe; keep your wits about you," he said. "I mean it about the door. Keep it bolted."

Amy nodded and placed her hand on Nick's arm. "All right, Will," she said. "But you keep safe as well."

Moments later, Will and Phoebe left, heading toward the stables, Will scanning the streets as his arm encircled Phoebe's shoulder. He repeatedly searched the road as the two left London, but Angus was nowhere in sight. Not until the two were on the way back to Chelsea did Will begin to relax.

Will and Phoebe slowed their horses as the cobbled London road turned to dirt. It had stopped snowing, and the snow they had passed through on their way into London now mixed with soil, creating brown sludge. Will slowed Baucent and took Phoebe's hand. "Let's do it," he said. "Let's get married."

"What?" Phoebe said.

"Let's get married, Phoebe. Seeing Angus today gave me a jolt. I'm sick of living in fear, of waiting for something to happen. So let's make something *good* happen! I want you, and I want to marry you. Rich and Angus be damned."

"I bring nothing to a marriage," Phoebe said. "I have no goods, no land, no family."

Will smiled. "You are all I care about."

"Will," Phoebe cautioned, then smiled. "Well then, yes."

Will grinned, grabbed Liard's reins, and led both horses toward a copse of trees hidden off the path. "What are you doing?" Phoebe said, laughing.

"Getting married!"

"Right now?"

"Right now."

THE FAILED APPRENTICE

Like many couples who lacked money or title, getting legally married was as easy as making vows to each other. No church was needed, nor officiate, nor witnesses. All it took were two willing participants, and Will and Phoebe were both willing. As they approached the thicket, Will dismounted and wrapped Baucent's reins around the branch of a plane tree, a leaf still clinging to its boughs. He helped Phoebe down and tethered Liard next to Baucent. Together, they walked into the small grove; in the center was a clearing, the ground a thin covering of untouched snow.

"Here," Will said. "If you'll have me, that is."

Phoebe smiled. "Of course."

Will faced Phoebe and took her hands in his. Her cheeks were rosy from the cold, and her eyes were warm. "In the eyes of God, I take you as my wife," Will said.

Phoebe squeezed Will's hand. "And in the eyes of God, I take you as my husband."

"Then we are married," Will said, laughing. "That was easy. Yet there is one thing left to make it binding."

Will took off his cape and lay it on the ground, causing a small whirlwind of snow to fly upwards and settle on the woolen cloak. He took Phoebe's hand as they knelt on the cape and kissed, their breath catching and quickening as they knew what was to come.

Will untied Phoebe's cape and let it fall to the ground. He struggled with the laces on her bodice; his hands were shaking and cold, and the laces were tied tight. "Let me," Phoebe said as she pulled on the top lace, loosening the bodice, which she then pushed to her waist. Will ran his hands over her warm breasts, their softness yielding to his hands, as Phoebe closed her eyes and leaned into him.

Will eased Phoebe back on the cloak as she reached for his breeches and pulled them below his hips. He moaned as her fingers found him; he grabbed a handful of her skirts and pulled them up and aside. Rolling on top of her, he parted her legs with his knees as she rose to meet him. Will had hoped their first time making love would be slow and on a feather bed, perhaps candles flickering against the walls, perhaps soft music surrounding them.

But it was not to be, neither the softness of a bed nor the speed at which Will hoped to perform. Moments later, he was inside her, and although he tried to move slowly, he found it impossible. And just like that, it was over.

Will rolled off Phoebe and smiled. "We will get used to each other this way," he said. "We will create our own rhythm. I'm sorry this time was so - quick."

Phoebe pulled up her bodice and adjusted her skirts. "It was good, Will," she said, smiling. "It didn't hurt like I've been told it would. You are gentle," she touched his arm. "So we are married," she said. "It's now official."

THE FAILED APPRENTICE

Chapter 24

Thomas More was not pleased with the news that the Roper girls' tutor had married their governess on the sly. "It may be legal," he said, scowling. "But marriage is a divine contract. You should be wed in a church. You should have followed ecclesiastical protocol."

Will smiled wryly. "Sir Thomas, forgive me for saying, but didn't you say that "love rules without rules?""

More laughed. "Very well, Will. Yes, I believe I did say that." Phoebe moved into Will's room that evening.

Will and Phoebe were not the only ones married that winter. In January, King Henry and Anne Boleyn were wed - perhaps for the second time - at Whitehall. Immediately following the wedding, Thomas Audley was appointed Lord Chancellor, Thomas More's former position. Audley was pro-reform, approved of King Henry's divorce from Katherine of Aragon, and supported his union with Anne Boleyn. More shook his head upon hearing the news. "England is falling into the devil's grasp," he confided in Will. "Satan is walking amongst us."

The cold wind blowing off the Thames began to abate at the end of March, and Will and Phoebe relished the softer air that heralded an early spring. Both had settled into married life easily and quickly, and, aside from silly jokes by the Roper girls and ribald comments by staff members, their life continued on a gentle trajectory. Angus appeared that late winter just a handful of times and seemed satisfied with the little information they provided him with. Will and Phoebe were confident that the details they passed along were relatively mild - nothing to damn the man who treated them like family.

More had also been generous in allowing Will and Phoebe to take time to spend in London with Amy and Nick. With each short visit, affection grew between Phoebe and her new family. She and Amy developed a sisterly bond, and Phoebe relished watching Amy's belly expand almost as much as Amy herself did.

Will had just finished his lessons with Lizzy and Meg one morning in late April; the sun was bright and the day unusually warm. Will looked out the window, content in his good fortune. He was married to a woman he loved, Amy's pregnancy was progressing well, and he was safe and well-fed. He smiled. Life was good. Then, from the corner of his eye, he saw Thomas More moving through the garden, engaged in a conversation with a young woman who was gesticulating wildly.

Will hurried down the stairs to the kitchen, where he found Mags elbow-deep in bread dough. "Who's that with Sir Thomas?" he asked.

"Oh," Mags' eyes became round. "Oh, Will. That's the Holy Maid of Kent, Elizabeth Barton."

Will had heard of Elizabeth Barton. An illiterate serving girl, Barton had begun to experience visions in 1527, often falling into fits where she claimed to be privy to a world beyond this one. Initially, Barton's prophesies denounced Protestantism, and she became lauded by the church and court. But soon, her visions took a darker turn. In late 1532, King Henry and Anne Boleyn visited her at Canterbury, where she wagged her finger at him and warned that if they were to marry, Henry's reign would be short, and he would die a "villain's death."

"You know she has visions," Mags continued. "I have heard that she thrashes around when she goes into a trance, and a voice comes from her belly."

Will thanked Mags for the information, left the kitchen, walked through the hall, and exited the house by the front door. The last thing he needed was Mags seeing him lurking around More, eavesdropping. But he'd like to get a good look at the prophet; he had seen Edward Thwaites' book chronicling her prophecies, *A Marvellous Work of Late Done at Court-of-Street*, in More's library.

Will took a circuitous route outside the house and through the garden, keeping low and hiding behind trees and hedges. More and Barton were heading to the chapel and Will followed, trying to remain unseen. Just as they neared the chapel doors, Will

THE FAILED APPRENTICE

stepped on a branch that snapped under his weight, the sound reverberating amongst the trees. More startled and whipped around; Will did his best to adopt a nonchalant demeanor. "Will!" More said. "You gave me a start."

Will's heart began hammering. "I was just out for a walk," he said, trying his best not to sound shifty. "It's a beautiful day."

"That it is," More replied. "Why don't you join us?"

Will sighed. Was More onto him? He had been so careful. Yet he and Phoebe thought they'd been careful as well. Yet he had no recourse. "I'd like that," he said, making his way through the heavy grass to More and Barton.

Elizabeth Barton was a petite woman, pale with flashing brown eyes. She wore a black tunic, befitting her role as a Benedictine nun. A black wimple hid her hair, although brown curls poked out at the corners. "Will, this is Elizabeth Barton. She's visiting from St. Sepulchre's in Canterbury."

"Sister Elizabeth," Will said, bowing his head.

"Come," More beckoned. "Elizabeth says she has some interesting news. We are going to the chapel to say a prayer. Then we will hear what she has to say."

Will followed More and Barton to the chapel and knelt with them at the altar. He watched as they both closed their eyes, their lips moving in prayer. He felt uneasy. How he wished he had been more diligent at remaining hidden.

"There," More said, bracing his hand against his knee as he stood. "Let's sit."

More, Barton, and Will sat on the chapel's hard benches that served as pews. "Elizabeth," More began. "Will is my granddaughters' tutor. But he has also become my friend. We enjoy discussing books. He has a sharp mind. I think he will be interested in what you have to say."

Barton nodded and stared at Will, her eyes penetrating. She knows, Will thought. She can see my deception.

"So," More began. "What do you have for me?"

"When the king was at Calais taking mass," she said, her voice surprisingly wispy. "I was there."

More looked at her questioningly. "I thought you were in Canterbury."

Barton rolled her eyes. "I was at Calais, but I was *invisible*. My physical being was in Canterbury, but my soul flew to Calais. Understand?"

More nodded. "Yes, of course. Go on."

"The king was about to accept the sacrament when an angel took it from the priest and gave it to me. That's how I know I am God's chosen messenger. And how I know that the king will be rejected by the church. His soul will be damned."

Will looked at More. There was no way that a man of such scholarship would believe Barton was an invisible presence in Calais. But More continued to watch her, nodding.

"I have seen the spot in Hell reserved for the king," she continued. "Now that he has married Boleyn, a great plague will sweep the land within six months. Be prepared. Shelter your family."

More sighed. "Anne Boleyn is going to be queen," he said. "You best watch what you say. As you know, it's illegal to even imagine the death of the king, much less say it. I would advise you to refrain from mentioning King Henry to anyone. It will not go well for you if you do."

"I am only concerned with my salvation and the salvation of England," Barton said.

"As am I," said More. "But still, mind yourself."

Barton stood up abruptly and glared at Will. "What do you have to say?" she demanded.

Will was shocked. "I'm listening," Will said, flustered. "I find your prophecies fascinating."

Barton squinted her eyes at Will. "I don't like you," she said. "I don't trust you."

More stood up. "Thank you for visiting, Elizabeth. I'm sure you best get going." He looked apologetically at Will.

Barton continued to glare at Will. "I will be going. It's a long ride back to Canterbury. But you best watch yourself, Master Will Patten. I see heartache coming for you. It's unavoidable."

THE FAILED APPRENTICE

More escorted Barton out of the chapel and to the stables, where she mounted a white horse. "Remember what I have said," she called as she rode away.

Once outside, Will breathed deeply. The woman was clearly unhinged, yet she did see something in me that eluded More for over a year, he thought.

"So, what do you think of our nun?" More said, catching up to Will.

"I'm a bit concerned she dislikes me so," Will said.

More laughed. "Elizabeth is a gifted prophet; that is indisputable. But don't set store by what she said about you. She doesn't like anyone."

"What she said about the king. It's treason."

"That it is," More said, nodding. "I told her again to watch her tongue. It could get her killed." Then: "Come with me. I have something for you and Phoebe. To commemorate your marriage."

Will followed More to his library, where he produced a small black velvet sack tied with a silk drawstring. More handed the bag to Will.

Will took the sack, which, alone, was more than he expected from More. He untied the black drawstring and pulled out a small book. The stiff leather covers were closed with silver clasps; the book was barely larger than his palm. Opening it, he gasped. "A Book of Hours," he said. "It's illuminated." The Book of Hours was a prayerbook that provided its readers text for daily prayer. Generally small, they were portable and could even be attached to a belt. Will flipped through the first few pages. Bordering the text were detailed drawings of animals, plants, and people. Surrounding the renderings were swirls and curlicues. The colors leapt from the page - cobalt blues, vivid yellows, deep reds.

Will reluctantly closed the book and handed it back to More. "I cannot accept this. It's too beautiful. It must be worth a fortune."

More waved his hand. "This? It's a trifle. What will I do with it, Will? I have a whole shelf of them."

Will doubted More had a whole shelf of such prized possessions but accepted the book. "Thank you, Sir Thomas. This is the nicest gift I've ever received."

More smiled, a genuine look of affection passing between him and Will. "Then treasure it and pass it to your children, which I hope will be many."

Will quailed at the thought of a household run wild with children, much like that of his parents, but smiled. To people, like More, who could afford it, many children were a blessing.

Phoebe was equally overwhelmed by the gift, tracing the intricate drawings with her index finger as she surveyed the book that evening. "We will treasure it," she said as she placed the book on the nightstand and climbed into bed next to Will. "More is a strange man - he can be so intractable, almost vicious. Yet to those he loves, he is kind and warm. Then there's the fanatical side to him."

"I had the strangest experience with him today," Will said as he recounted the odd conversation with Elizabeth Barton, including her penetrating glare, treasonous talk, and her unsettling prophecy.

"You don't believe that nonsense," Phoebe said.

"More thinks she's divine," Will replied.

"More thinks a lot of things," Phoebe said. "He thinks a hair shirt will make him a better Catholic. He thinks whipping himself will bring him closer to God."

"I don't know," Will said. "That stare of hers. It was like she could see my soul. She *knew*, Phoebe. She knew what we've been up to."

"You really don't believe that, Will."

Will shrugged his shoulders. Perhaps the Holy Maid was right. Perhaps heartache was just around the corner. So much to worry about, Will thought as he drifted off to sleep. Amy, pregnant. Rich breathing down his neck. And the ever-present threat of Angus.

THE FAILED APPRENTICE

Chapter 25

In late May, two couriers arrived at More's home within hours of each other. One came with the news that Amy had delivered a healthy, if premature, baby boy named Thomas. Amy had survived the delivery, and mother and child were healthy. Will breathed a sigh of relief; he was all too aware of the dangers of childbirth to both mother and infant. The second courier arrived for More with less happy news. Archbishop Cranmer had declared King Henry's marriage to Katherine of Aragon invalid in the eyes of the church. Stephen Gardiner had been immediately dispatched to Marseilles to meet with the Pope and King Francis on King Henry's behalf. And King Henry was waiting on More's reply - would he attend Anne Boleyn's coronation on June 1st?

"You go see your sister and nephew," More said to Will. "But I will remain in Chelsea. I will not attend that coronation."

"Are you sure, Sir Thomas?" Will asked. "Forgive me, but the king may take this as a snub."

More shrugged his shoulders. "King Henry is free to take it as he wishes," he replied. "I have drawn the line. I will not go."

Will left the next morning for London, anxious to see Amy and her new family but reluctant to leave Phoebe in Chelsea. Yet a nephew! Will couldn't wait to hold the baby, to see the Patten line reflected in the infant's tiny face.

The ride to St. Botolph's Lane was easy, but as he approached London, the streets became crowded, hucksters lining the road. The coronation, Will thought. These people are here to see the new queen.

Will navigated Baucent through the crowds, Baucent getting more agitated as he was forced to sidestep carriages, riders, and aggressive merchants. It took Will twice as long to get to Amy and Nick's home as it normally would.

Leaving Baucent at the nearby stable, Will anxiously walked to the Greenes', a tight grasp on his saddlebag. He heard the baby's cries as soon as he turned onto the lane. The screams ratcheted up as he approached the house, and by the time he was at Amy and Nick's doorstep, the infant was at full screech. Will tried the door; it was not bolted. He had warned Amy and Nick about keeping the door secure - were they not taking his advice seriously? He opened the latch and walked in. Amy sat on a chair next to the hearth, holding the red-faced infant in her arms. She looked at Will and began to sob.

"He won't stop crying," Amy said. "All day, all night! He never stops!"

Will walked over and took the baby from Amy, the infant's back arching as Will held him, his tiny fists bunched in angry round balls. "Hello there, Tom," Will said. Tom replied by screaming even louder. "The door was unbolted," Will began, turning to Amy. "I thought I told you…."

"Thank God you are here," Amy interrupted, pushing the hair off her face with the back of her hand. "Since Gardiner left for France, Nick is never home. Gardiner saddled Nick with even more to do than usual."

Will tried to bounce Tom on his shoulder, something he had seen his mother do with his siblings. It had worked for them, but not so with this baby. "At least Gardiner didn't bring Nick with him," he said. He would broach the subject of the door bolt later.

"Oh, I wouldn't stand for that," Amy laughed tiredly. "Nick knows better than to even bring that up."

Will held the baby in front of him, searching for traces of Amy or Nick on his angry little face. Tom's eyes were shut tightly, tiny tears trickling out of their corners. His toothless mouth opened, letting out a tired cry. "I think he has your nose," Will said. "And our father's temper."

"You really can't tell what he looks like right now," Amy said. "The few seconds he's asleep, he looks a lot like Nick. But right now, he just looks like a red-faced little rogue."

Will laughed, walked over, and placed Tom in his cradle. It was beautifully carved with images of animals and flowers lining the sides. A soft cotton blanket was balled up in the corner, a dollop

THE FAILED APPRENTICE

of vomit stuck to its center. "The cradle was Nick's," Amy said, rolling her bloodshot eyes. "All the Greene babies use it. Just like all the first-born Greene boys are named "Thomas.""

Will noted irritation in Amy's voice. "Is everything all right between you two?" he asked.

"Fine," Amy said, the vestige of a smile on her face. "Nick is a good husband and father. I'm just exhausted. Mistress Chapman - Lucy - tries to help, but she's almost blind. So really, no real help at all."

"Go to bed; get some sleep," Will said. "I'll watch this little terror. And bathe while you're at it."

Amy smiled. "Thank you, Will. Those are the kindest words I've heard all day. Which tells you what kind of day I've been having."

Amy stood, stretched her back, and walked into the bedchamber before Will could change his mind. Tom was still crying, but his screeches had turned into whimpers. Will rocked the cradle with his foot, wondering if he and Phoebe would have children soon and if they'd exact the same toll this little creature was taking on his mother.

Nick arrived home just as the sun was beginning to set. "Will," he said, surprised at his friend's presence in his home. "I see you've met your nephew."

Tom saw his father and let out a shriek. "Take him, please," Will said, removing Tom from the cradle and handing him to his father. "He did sleep - for about a minute. Since then, he's been fussing and whining. I've held him, rocked him - nothing seems to work. Amy is sleeping, although how she can rest through this noise is beyond me."

Nick looked at the angry infant, who seemed to be giving him the evil eye. "He's hungry and wet. Let me take him to Amy, then we can talk."

Nick disappeared with Tom into the bedroom. Will could hear a quiet conversation begin between Nick and Amy, then the baby's cries stopped. He must be nursing, Will thought. At last, some peace.

Nick returned and poured two tankards of ale from a pitcher on the sideboard. He handed one to Will and downed his in one long draw. He leaned back in his chair and sighed. "You look good, Will. Marriage seems to agree with you. We meant to get you and Phoebe a wedding gift but," he waved his hand around the room, "this."

"I understand," Will said. "No gift necessary."

The two sat quietly for a moment, then Nick filled Will in on his duties since Gardiner had been dispatched to France. "Accompany me to the coronation procession tomorrow," he said. "I'll have a good seat, thanks to Gardiner."

"Should you leave Amy?" Will asked.

"Lucy is coming tomorrow to help, so it's best I'm not here. I'll just get in the way." Will recalled Amy's comment about Lucy's lack of help but said nothing.

The following day was perhaps the grandest of the four-day coronation spectacle. Anne Boleyn had been staying at the royal apartments in the Tower of London and would process from the Tower to Westminster Hall. Close to 300 members of nobility and clergy joined the procession as it moved slowly through London's streets, the crowds gathering to get their first gawk at the new queen. Will and Nick walked northward to Gracechurch Street, where Nick assured Will a spot was reserved for them. They arrived at an elevated gallery where a man in royal livery stood, demanding a ticket for them to gain access to the seats above.

"I'm Nick Greene," Nick said proudly. "I'm here on orders of Bishop Gardiner. Please let us pass."

"Never heard of you," the official said. "You need a ticket to pass. Now move along."

"I'm Nick *Greene,*" Nick tried again. "Stephen Gardiner? The Bishop of Winchester? He sent me."

"You could be Nick Yellow for all I care," the man replied. "You won't be getting in without a ticket."

Nick shook his fist at the much larger man. "You don't want to get on the wrong side of Gardiner," he said. "I'll remember this."

THE FAILED APPRENTICE

"See that you do," the guard said as he took Nick by the shoulder and pushed him into the street, where Nick fell into a fresh pile of horse manure.

Will helped Nick up as Nick tried to shake the ordure from his cloak. "God's wounds!" he spat out. "I don't understand this. Gardiner said he'd have a spot for me."

Will pulled Nick to the side of the road, which had been covered in gravel to prevent the processing horses from slipping. "No matter. We can see fine from here."

"Now I smell like horse shit," Nick said. "If I meet the queen, that's how she'll remember me."

"I don't think you need to worry about that," Will said, surveying the crowd swelling along the street. "Let's get a drink while we wait."

Fountains throughout the city spouted wine in celebration of the queen's coronation, and Will and Nick filled their mugs and found a spot on the side of the road to sit. The buildings surrounding them were festooned with arras and tapestries, and onlookers hung precariously from the windows. Despite the tumult of Anne Boleyn's rise to the crown, the population that afternoon was loud, happy, and celebratory.

"I heard More isn't coming," Nick said as he tried to make himself comfortable on the curb. "The king is none too pleased."

"He won't come," Will replied. "That's one concession he will not make."

"It will come back to bite him," Nick said. "You can be sure."

Will sighed. "He's intractable. You know my story, Amy's story. Our own parents have rejected us. More has been like a father to me. Yet I remember the zeal as he watched heretics burn on the pyre. I can't reconcile the kind family man to the man stomping on Richard Bayfield's ashes."

"It's his faith," Nick said after a moment. "He has beliefs, as unyielding as they may be. There's something to be said for a man who won't compromise, who knows when to say here is a line, I will not cross it."

Will took a long drink of wine and looked at Nick. "Your door. It was unbolted. I hoped I had made clear how important it is for you to keep the door secured."

"What's this all about? Who cares if our door is latched? We have very little of value to steal."

Will sighed. Guilt and fear lay heavy on his shoulders. "Rich wants me to get information on More and to pass it along to him. He's blackmailing me, Nick. His henchman is threatening me, and if I don't do as he wants, he's threatened you and Amy as well."

"So that's why you want us to bolt the door," Nick said, nodding.

"Which Amy has not done."

"If he really wanted to get to us, a bolted door won't keep him out," Nick said. "But do you really think there's danger? I mean, what has Rich to gain by hurting us?"

"I don't know, Nick. Leverage. To create fear. I'm at the point where I don't know what to do."

Nick paused for a moment, thinking. "You are a good man, Will. A good friend, a good brother, and a good husband. Think about what you value. I know you love Amy and me. But don't let your fear for us destroy you. Don't sell your soul. We will be fine."

Will nodded. "It's killing me, Nick."

Nick laid his hand on Will's shoulder. "Where will it end, Will? Only you can decide how much you're willing to take. How many compromises you're willing to make. I can't make that choice for you."

As Will opened his mouth to reply, a whoop went up from the crowd; the procession had begun to pass, and Will and Nick scrambled to their feet. Nobles and knights, walking two by two, marched by, followed by judges and Knights of the Bath, wearing violet robes. Then came higher governmental and ecclesiastical officials on horseback. Will saw Rich riding in front of Cromwell, resplendent in a scarlet mantle draped across his horse's back. As if sensing Will's presence, Rich cast his eyes in Will's direction

THE FAILED APPRENTICE

and raised an eyebrow. He nodded almost imperceptibly, shifted his gaze forward, and continued his progression.

The crowds continued to swell and jostle as the queen approached. A middle-aged woman pushed into Will. "I had to see this for meself," the woman said, letting out a loud belch. She swayed and grabbed Will's arm. "I need to see the whore our king put aside his rightful wife for." She leaned close to Will, her breath stinking of old ale and wine.

"Mistress, you best keep your opinions to yourself," Will said, extracting the woman's claw-like grip from his arm. But the woman's displeasure made Will aware of those around him. So not everyone is happy, he thought. Some men still wore their caps as Anne Boleyn began to pass; some turned their backs.

The queen sat in a white satin litter pulled by two horses dressed from head to haunch in white damask. Will got his first look at Anne Boleyn. She was obviously pregnant and dressed in a white surcoat interwoven with gold threads and an ermine mantle. Her dark hair cascaded down her shoulders, past her waist, and a gold circlet sat upon her head, its jewels sparkling in the fading sunlight. Above her head was a canopy made from cloth of gold with tiny silver bells, although Will could not hear their jingling from the swell of noise from the crowds.

"She ain't nothing to see," the drunken woman said, turning her attention to Nick. "In my day, I was a real beauty," she burped again. "Not like that strumpet."

Nick looked over the woman's head at Will and rolled his eyes. The queen had passed, and now her ladies processed by, all riding chariots and dressed in crimson. Further down the street at Leadenhall, a tableau had been created for the queen to enjoy. But they could see little from their perch on Gracechurch Street.

Will turned to Nick, who was still being harangued by the drunken woman. "And another thing," she said as she poked a fat finger at Nick's chest. "King Henry…," she began as she suddenly blanched, pressed her hand against her stomach, and threw up on Nick. "Ah, that's better," she said.

"God damn it, woman!" Nick said, pushing her away. Unfazed, the woman staggered off in the direction of the nearest fountain of wine. Nick turned to Will. "Let's get out of here," he said. "I smell like shit and vomit."

It took them a while to get back to St. Botolph's Lane, and when Nick tried the door, it swung open easily. Will looked at Nick and shook his head. "Bolt the door," he said.

THE FAILED APPRENTICE

Chapter 26

Three weeks later, Angus came for a visit. Will and Phoebe were walking along the Thames, enjoying the warmth of the late June afternoon. Sunlight twinkled on the river, and wherries bobbed lazily on the water. A soft breeze blew, rustling Phoebe's skirt, a gift from Alice More.

"If it isn't the lovebirds," Angus snarled as he rode up behind Will and Phoebe. "Just who I've come to see."

Will startled. "What do you want?" he said.

Angus dismounted his horse and grabbed the reins. "You know what I want."

"We have nothing for you," Will said.

"I don't think that's true," Angus replied. "I think there's been goings-on here in the last month or so that you haven't reported. Things that you should have let Master Rich know about."

"If you already know something, then you don't need us," Will said.

"Now Will, you know that's not right. We need information, first-hand information. My master doesn't dabble in hearsay." He paused, then looked at Phoebe. "Mistress Patten? What say you?"

"I don't know anything, Angus," Phoebe said. "I agree with my husband."

Angus made a show of taking a deep breath and exhaling slowly. "Your nephew, Thomas, isn't it? I understand he is a cute boy but born a bit early. Babies born early tend not to survive, eh?"

"Don't even," Will seethed. Phoebe looked panicked.

"Just stating a fact, Will. It would be a shame if something happened to that little boy. Fevers are so easy to catch these days."

Will felt heat rise to his face. There would always be something, wouldn't there? First, he was the target. Then Amy. Now Tom. The answer came to him as quickly as the bile rising in his throat. He knew there would be no end. As long as he allowed Angus to bully him, to threaten him, there would always be a sister, a baby, a son or a daughter for Angus to target. "No information," Will said.

"Will!" Phoebe said, grabbing his arm. Her eyes were wild.

"No information, Angus. Take that back to Rich and Cromwell. We cannot help you."

"Really, Will?" Angus said. "You'd sacrifice your own nephew for More? Your own blood for that papist?" Angus shook his head. "I thought you were better than that."

Will knew what he could do - tell Angus about Elizabeth Barton's visit, the treasonous dialogue between her and More, and More's refusal to attend the coronation. But to what end? To go through this charade again a month from now? A year? A lifetime? More had been kind to him; More deserved better than to be served up on a plate to Rich and Cromwell. He'd get a message to Nick. He'd make sure Nick knew what to watch for. "No sacrifice, Angus," he said. "There is nothing to report."

"Have it your way, Will. I hope you had a fine last look at your nephew when you visited for the coronation." Angus mounted his horse, who kicked at the ground.

"Wait, Angus!" Phoebe lurched at Angus' reins and held them fast. "Will, tell him something, anything!"

Angus sneered. "Listen to your wife."

Will looked at Angus astride his horse. Angus' eyes flashed with cruel pleasure. He's enjoying this, Will thought. "I told you, there is nothing to report," Will looked at his wife, clutching the reins, her eyes darting between him and Angus. "Let's go, Phoebe. Let him tell Rich what he wants." Will turned and started walking back to More's home.

"You will regret this, you piece of shit," Angus yelled after him.

Will ignored Angus and continued down the road, his eyes filling with tears, his hands shaking. He had taken a stand, but had he also condemned his infant nephew to an early grave? His stomach roiled, and he bent over and vomited next to the path. A cold sweat broke out on Will's face, and he braced his hands on his knees, staring at the dirt road that led from Chelsea to London.

THE FAILED APPRENTICE

He heaved again, coughing, and wiping his mouth with the back of his hand. The Thames lapped gently to his left. How easy it would be, he thought, just to walk into the river, to sink, to be done with this life.

Moments later, Phoebe ran up behind Will. "My God," she said. "Will, look at you!"

Will collapsed into Phoebe's arms. She rubbed his back as he let sobs overtake him. "I had to end this, Phoebe," he said. "It simply can't go on."

Phoebe cradled his head in her hands. "Angus is gone," she said. "Let's get back home, get you cleaned up. What's done is done."

Will could not sleep that night. He couldn't eat, for that matter, nor sit still. At supper, he watched Thomas More, surrounded by his family, his favorite child Margaret, his wealthy wife Alice, Lizzy and Meg climbing all over him. Did I just sacrifice it all, he thought, for this man who has everything?

That night Will lay awake as Phoebe snored quietly, curled up in their bed. He stared out the window at the sky, the moon and stars obscured by heavy clouds. A soft summer breeze blew in and ruffled the light sheet covering him. The air smelled like rain, like a brewing storm. Although his gut twisted from the events of the afternoon, on some level, there was peace. He had drawn a line and not crossed it; he still had a vestige of his soul. Thomas More had taught him that.

Will resolved he would leave in the morning and warn Nick and Amy about Angus. He'd make them move, if only for a while. Perhaps they could return to Chelsea with him and stay at More's home. There was certainly enough room. At worst, they could lay low at the Axe. He was sure Ellyn could find them a safe place to hide. Or maybe Nick could follow Gardiner to France? Angus couldn't get to him there.

With options and a resolution to act on them, Will fell into a fitful sleep. His dreams were dark and violent, and he awoke in a panic. Phoebe continued to sleep as dawn broke and the storm promised in the night arrived. The wind picked up and blew through the open window, rain drenching the floor. As Will rose to close the window, a shard of lightning split the sky, followed by a crack and the roar of thunder. Yet Phoebe slept on. How could she sleep so soundly, Will wondered. How can she act as though yesterday didn't matter?

The storm was violent and lasted most of the day, preventing Will from traveling to London. Boughs came down in the orchard, and lightning struck the tree where More had tied and whipped heretics, where Will and Phoebe had shared a passionate moment, blackening the trunk and opening a deep swath of earth beneath it, exposing the roots. Will spent the morning teaching the Roper girls but was distracted, upset that the storm delayed his trip to London. If it was this bad in Chelsea, surely London felt the storm equally. Angus would not go out in such a tempest, would he? Maybe this bought Will some time.

The following day broke clear, the air fresh, the wind light. Will awoke and prepared to leave for London. The roads were sure to be muddy; he pulled on his old leather boots that had seen plenty of dirt and grime. He would try and get to London before Nick left for Winchester Palace.

Will kissed Phoebe goodbye, telling her the girls would have no lessons that morning. He headed across the expanse of lawn to the stables, sidestepping fallen branches and puddles. He felt light. Nick and Amy would move their small family away from Angus' menacing grasp. They would come up with a plan once they were together.

Will led Baucent from the stables, giving him a carrot he swiped from the kitchen. He watched the horse eat, his teeth large and jaw strong. Will rubbed the horse's neck and traced Baucent's scar. Despite enduring horrors Will could only imagine, Baucent had become a gentle, compliant companion.

Once secure on his horse's saddle, Will rode down More's lane, Baucent's lower legs already muddy from the puddles cratering the road. He passed More's house, its grand facade facing the Thames, the front gardens in bloom. Turning onto the road heading to London, a group of men rode swiftly toward him. Will moved Baucent to let the group pass.

THE FAILED APPRENTICE

But they did not pass. Instead, they turned into More's lane, barely slowing their pace. There were five of them, and at the head of the group was Cromwell, with Rich at his heels. Will did not recognize the other men, but Angus wasn't one of them. Will locked eyes with Rich, who smiled as he passed.

Cromwell and his cronies dismounted their horses, climbed the steps to More's house, and banged on the door. Will inched Baucent closer and saw Mags open the door, Cromwell push past her, followed by Rich and their lackeys. Will felt the prickle of panic; he dismounted Baucent and ran toward the house.

Alice More stood in the hall, hands on her hips. "You," she pointed at Cromwell, her hand shaking. "Take you and your group of flunkeys and get out of my home!"

"Not without your husband," Cromwell said. "And I'd advise you not to point that finger at me unless you want to lose it."

Will glanced at Rich, who gave him a half-smile. "You best listen to Master Cromwell," Rich said, puffing out his chest.

Thomas More appeared at the top of the staircase. "What is the meaning of this?" he said as he slowly walked down the stairs, eyeing the group gathered below, assessing the tension filling the room. "I don't appreciate raised voices in my home."

Cromwell walked up to More and met him at the base of the staircase. "Thomas More," he said, acid dripping from his voice. "You are under arrest. You best come with me."

Will looked at More, panicked. Yet More barely reacted. "And what might the charges be?" he asked.

"Treason, to start," Rich piped in.

"Treason?" More said. "Why, I am nothing but a loyal servant to King Henry."

Cromwell laughed. "You opposed the king's marriage. You do not recognize the king as head of the church. You have been cavorting with that witch Barton, speaking with her of the king's death. Need I go on, Thomas?"

More nodded. "I have been quiet on the king's position as head of the church. And no law in the world can punish any man for his silence."

"Enough," Cromwell said, grabbing More by the arm. "You will have plenty of time to think about this in the Tower."

More retained his composure. "I would like a moment to gather some things," he said.

"Thomas!" Alice More said, grabbing More's sleeve. "You will not be going with these men!"

"Have someone bring your *things* to the Tower later," Cromwell said, ignoring Alice More. "You're to come with us now. Don't make this harder than it need be, Thomas."

"Very well," More sighed. Then he turned to Alice. "Tell William to come to the Tower this afternoon. He'll know what to do." For a moment, Will thought More was referring to him, but it didn't take more than a beat to realize he was speaking of William Roper, Margaret's husband.

Alice let out a sob and clung to More. "Thomas, say whatever you need to survive. I will not have you taken from me."

More pushed her back. "My soul is safe, Alice, and I'll try and keep my body safe as well. Do not worry," he said as he allowed Cromwell to lead him from the house.

Once More was gone, the horses' hoofbeats fading to silence, Alice collapsed in a chair. She turned to Will. "I knew that man's principles would be his undoing," she said, wiping her eyes. Mags handed her a handkerchief which she used to blow her nose. "I told him to keep quiet. He wouldn't listen."

Margaret Roper appeared at the top of the stairs and flew down the steps, her sobs reverberating through the hall. "I heard them take Father away," she sobbed and threw herself at Alice's feet.

"Margaret, get up," Alice said, not unkindly. "Have your husband prepare to go to the Tower. He and Thomas can figure out where to go from there."

Will stood in the hall, feeling awkward as this family tableau unfolded. He turned to leave, to head to London, but looked up and saw Phoebe standing at the top of the stairs. She met Will's eyes and turned away.

The look on Phoebe's face told Will all he needed to know. He raced up the stairs two at a time and followed Phoebe into their

THE FAILED APPRENTICE

bedchamber. "What have you done?" he said, staring at her incredulously.

Phoebe sat heavily on the bed. "You left me no choice," she said. "I had to tell Angus. I had to tell him what you'd told me. About Barton, about the treason."

"You had to tell him *nothing*!" Will hissed, trying to keep his voice level.

"I did, Will! He was threatening little Tom. I couldn't let anything happen to him; he's a baby! And I can't believe you would."

"Nothing was going to happen to Tom! I would have made sure of it."

Phoebe laughed sadly. "I love you, Will. But I don't think you could win in a fight against Angus." She sighed and met his eyes. "Amy, Nick, Tom - they're my family too. I will do what I must to protect them. Even if that means dealing with Angus. And they are safe, thanks to me."

"But More - he's been like a father to us. He's treated us with nothing but kindness. They've hauled him to the Tower on treason charges. Also, thanks to you."

"I am sorry for More. But he's not my family. You are. Amy is. Nick is. And little Tom is, too. They're more important to me than Thomas More."

Will looked at Phoebe - an orphan who, like Will, did what she had to do to survive. And he understood the importance family held for her. It was powerful, all-encompassing. "You've condemned More to death," Will finally said, and an image of the heads on London Bridge flashed across his mind.

"I don't think so. He'll recant and accept King Henry as head of the church."

"You don't know More," said Will. "He will do neither."

"Then I'm sorry for that."

Will sat on the bed next to Phoebe. "I had to take a stand against Angus, Phoebe. I had to end the threats, the bullying. And you undid it all."

"You did what you had to do. So did I," Phoebe said, taking Will's hand. "I did what I needed to do to protect this family. And I'd do it again."

Will opened his mouth to speak, but a clamor arose from the stairs, and Mags appeared in the door, out of breath. "Will, your horse is outside, trampling the flowers and braying to wake the dead. You best come and get him. There's enough chaos this morning without a loose horse to deal with."

Will had forgotten about Baucent, who he had left in front of More's house. He sighed. "This discussion is not over," he said to Phoebe as he followed Mags down the stairs and past a stone-faced Alice More.

Baucent was, indeed, raising a ruckus in the front yard, pawing at the ground, digging up flowers, and chewing on the peppermint that grew like a weed next to the house. Will crept up behind him and grabbed the horse's reins as Baucent turned and gave him the side-eye. "Your moment of freedom is over," Will said. "I know you're confused by everything that's going on. So am I."

Will took the reins and led Baucent around the house to the stables, handing him off to Rory. But as Rory took the reins, Baucent reared back and showed his teeth, his wild eyes looking past Will to the stable doors. Rory held tight to the reins as Will whipped around. Angus stood in the doorway, the sun backlighting him in a dark silhouette.

Angus walked into the stable as Baucent began to kick and pull on his reins. "Get out of here," Will said. "You have what you want. What are you even doing here?"

Angus approached Baucent, who was stomping his hooves and braying. "I followed Masters Cromwell and Rich, just to be sure they didn't need my," he paused, weighing his words, "expertise. I lingered in the background, watching. I'm good at that, as you know. They didn't even know I was there," he said, pompously. "Since I'm here, I thought I'd thank your pretty little wife in person for her information. The information *you* should have given me. She saved your skin." Angus laughed darkly and

THE FAILED APPRENTICE

moved to stroke Baucent's neck, his hand hovering above the horse's scar.

"Keep away from my wife and my horse," Will said as Rory fought to control Baucent.

Angus smirked. "Oh, you're a fearsome one," he said, laughing. "I'm quaking in my boots."

As Angus leaned in to touch Baucent's neck, the horse reared. Angus stumbled back, and Baucent wrenched free of Rory and his grasp on the reins. Baucent reared again, his front hoof connecting with Angus' skull, the crack resounding through the stables as Angus collapsed. Angus lay on the stable floor, immobile, as Baucent reared a third time, his hoof landing heavily on Angus' chest.

Angus gasped, blood bubbling from his lungs and streaming from his mouth. He coughed once, twice, blood flying from his lips and landing on Baucent's legs. As he took his last breath, Baucent calmed, walked a few steps to Will, and nuzzled his shoulder. Rory looked at Will, wide-eyed, as he grabbed Baucent's reins. Angus' body lay crumpled in the stable's hay, blood still dribbling down his chin.

"The cur deserved it," Rory said, his voice shaking. "It wasn't Baucent's fault. That arse had been tormenting him. You can be sure of that."

Will looked at Angus' crumpled body and felt nothing but fear that he and Rory would be held accountable for the lout's deserved demise, that Angus would finally have what he wanted all along: Will destroyed. "I will not pay for this," Will said. "Neither will you." He paused for a moment, thinking. Angus had said he was here, under his own volition and undetected. That was helpful. "The tree, the old one in the back of the orchard," Will said, waving vaguely at the area behind More's house. "You know the one I mean?"

"The old oak? The whipping tree?' Rory said.

"Yes. The storm opened the ground by it," Will said. "Wide enough to fit a man." He looked pointedly at Rory.

It took Rory a moment, but soon he nodded. "I'll get my brother. We'll bury the body tonight. My brother works in Sir Thomas' gardens; I'll have him bring his spade."

"In the meantime, let's get the body out of the way," Will said, walking to Angus' feet and picking them up, dragging the body toward a horse stall. "He can stay here until nightfall."

Rory nodded again. "My brother and I got this. No one will be the wiser."

"Come get me if you need me," Will said, wiping his hands on his breeches, making sure he was free of blood splatter.

"My brother's strong. We should make short work of this one." Rory motioned at Angus' lifeless form.

"You're a good man, Rory."

"I don't condone killing," Rory said. "But this man, he was evil. Some men just shouldn't live."

Will nodded. He had come across a few like this in his short life.

THE FAILED APPRENTICE

Chapter 27

Will felt no guilt over Angus' death but experienced overwhelming sadness over More's arrest. He watched as William Roper left for the Tower later that morning, cluelessly retrieving his horse from Rory at the stable. Roper returned that evening, exhausted and demoralized. More was being held in the Bell Tower. With its eleven-foot thick stone walls, the Bell Tower was reserved for the most distinguished prisoners. More was allowed books, pens, and paper which Roper would bring him the following day. Will asked if he could accompany him to see More. "I'd be happy for you to join me," Roper said. "But I have business in London, so after the visit, you're on your own."

Will had no problem with that, and the pair loaded four saddlebags with candles, blankets, books, and writing materials. As Will approached the stables, Rory nodded to him. He looked past Rory at the swath of earth by the whipping tree. It was filled with fresh dirt. There was little sign of the disrupted ground, no evidence of a hidden body.

The Tower was as formidable as Will remembered, and he shivered recalling his brief stay in the dark, rodent-infested dungeon, which seemed like a lifetime ago. But as he walked up the stone steps that led to More's cell, he realized that More was staying in much better conditions. Will and Roper stopped when they reached the heavy, iron-studded door that opened to More's cell. The entrance was guarded by two men in yeomen warder livery, holding sharpened partisans.

"We're here to see Thomas More," Roper said.

"He is not allowed visitors," one of the guards replied.

"I have his supplies," Roper responded, opening the saddlebags for inspection. The guard peered in and rifled through the bags. "And something for your troubles." Roper handed each guard a gold coin.

"Very well, be quick about it," the guard said as he opened More's door with a heavy iron key.

A blast of cold air hit Will as he entered More's pentagonal cell. Even though it was a warm summer day, the cell was icy. The room's arrow-slit windows offered the only view of the outside world and the only access to fresh air. Threadbare rugs lined the stone floor but added no warmth to the room. Tallow candles flickered in niches, casting little light. More was seated at a small desk, a prayer book in his hands. He stood when he saw his visitors; Roper walked over and embraced his father-in-law while Will held back.

"Will, come here," More said, and he wrapped Will in a hug. "It was good of you to come. I'm sorry I can't offer you food and wine." More smiled, but his eyes were sad.

"We brought you some things," Roper said as he began to unpack the saddlebags, stacking books and paper on the small desk. "They'll let you write letters. I have quill pens and ink, paper too. I also brought wool blankets. It was freezing in here yesterday."

"Thank you," More said, steadying the books teetering on the desk with his hand.

"We'll get you out of here," Roper said. "They can't prove anything."

More sighed. "I'm here for a while, William. They won't let me out anytime soon. I understand that Cromwell and Rich will be conducting interviews with me. I just hope I'm not put on the rack."

Will was shocked. "They wouldn't dare," he said. "You're *Thomas More*, not some common criminal."

More shrugged his shoulders. "I've known Rich for most of my life," he said. "The man had a questionable reputation even when he was young. He was a dicer; he played fast and loose with the truth. And Cromwell, well, he's a brute. So who knows? I'm trying to prepare myself for that eventuality."

One of the guards poked his head into More's cell. "Wrap it up," he said.

THE FAILED APPRENTICE

"Just do what you must to get out of here," Roper said. "Sign whatever they put in front of you. Lie if you must. Just come home. This vermin-riddled place can't be good for your health."

More sighed. "Is my home in Chelsea closer to Heaven than this cell? I think not."

"You're exasperating," Roper said and hugged his father-in-law.

"That I am," More said. Then he turned to Will. "I've enjoyed getting to know you, Will. I hope you continue reading and learning." He walked over and patted Will on the shoulder. "And take care of your wife."

Will and Roper left the Tower, Will sensing that this would be the last time he would see More alive. "I'm heading to Lincoln's Inn. I'll see you back in Chelsea," Roper said as he mounted his jennet and, without looking back, rode away from the Tower.

Will had some time before heading back; he considered visiting Amy but felt restless. His time with More had left him unsettled. As much as he'd like to see Tom, the thought of holding a crying baby while his head was swimming was unappealing. As he stood next to Baucent, trying to figure out his next move, he heard a voice from behind. "Well done, Will." Will turned around to see Rich approaching. "It took you a while, but we got him."

"You can't torture him," Will said. "You can't kill him."

Rich shrugged his shoulders. "It's up to More now."

Will looked at Rich - a pompous man lacking any moral fiber. "I am done," Will said. "I've done what you've asked and more."

Rich cocked his head. "Perhaps."

"Done," Will said as he mounted Baucent.

Rich grabbed Baucent's reins. "I see you, Will. I see what you're made of. You may think you're done, but are you really?"

Will held Rich's gaze. "I'm not like you," he said.

"Are you sure about that?"

"Let go of my horse."

Rich continued to hang onto Baucent's reins. "The scales between us are balanced, Will. I consider your debt paid. But I don't think our history is completely written. You know where to find me." Rich let go of the reins, and Will turned Baucent toward the street. "I'll see you soon," Rich said as Will rode away.

Will turned and looked back once he left the Tower grounds. Rich still stood in the shade of a yew tree, a smirk on his face. Rich raised his hand and waved at Will, and Will felt a chill pass through him. Will remembered Culler swinging from the gallows. He recalled Angus lying in a heap in the stables. He had shown no mercy, no sorrow, for neither man nor believed they warranted any. But Will was nothing like Rich - nothing. Yet fate could be cruel, and he already felt an invisible tether tying him to Richard Rich. He turned away and headed back to Chelsea, trying to dismiss the sense of unease gnawing at his gut.

THE FAILED APPRENTICE

Author's Note

Many individuals featured in *The Failed Apprentice* were real. Certainly, Thomas More was, and I have taken liberties with the timeline of his arrest. In reality, More was arrested for treason on April 17, 1534, about nine months after he met a similar fate in the book. He was found guilty, based partially on questionable testimony from Richard Rich, and beheaded on July 1, 1535 at Tower Hill. More's head was displayed on London Bridge and ultimately rescued by his daughter, Margaret Roper. It is believed the head is buried in the Roper Vault of St Dunstan's Church, Canterbury. His hair shirt survived and can be seen at Buckfast Abbey in Devon. Sadly, nothing remains of More's home in Chelsea. However, a section of his chapel exists as part of Chelsea Old Church in London.

Elizabeth Barton was a real person who was known as "The Nun of Kent," "The Holy Maid of London," "The Holy Maid of Kent," and later "The Mad Maid of Kent." She professed to having visions and was taken seriously by Henry VIII and his court. Arrested in November of 1533, examined by Thomas Cromwell and Thomas Cranmer and possibly tortured, Barton ultimately recanted her prophesies and confessed that her visions had been faked. In January of 1534, Barton was accused of treason and hanged at Tyburn. She was 28 years old.

Richard Rich was a real person, as was Thomas Cromwell. Rich was known as Cromwell's ruthless henchman who was not above torturing people to get information. He married Elizabeth Jenkes in the mid-1530s and had fifteen children with her. Whereas Elizabeth Jenkes was real, Phillippa, Maud, and John Jenkes were not.

Heretics Richard Bayfield and James Bainham were both real, and both burned at the stake, a punishment in which More was directly involved.

W.J. SMALL

Stephen Gardiner was real and managed to survive Henry VIII's reign. He became Lord Chancellor under Queen Mary I and died at the age of 72.

Many other characters sprung from my imagination, including Ellyn, Hugh Culler, Angus, and Nick Greene. Phoebe Houghton, although not real, was named after my 12th great-grandmother.

I owe special thanks to several resources and people. First, Peter Ackroyd's *The Life of Thomas More* was invaluable in learning about this complex man's life. E.J. Burford's *The Bishop's Brothels* gave an in-depth look at Southwark's brothels in the 16th century. *The Faithful Executioner: Life and Death, Honor and Shame in the Turbulent Sixteenth Century* by Joel F. Harrington was a fascinating view of execution methods and the role of the hangman in both society and at the gallows. I am likewise indebted to *A New Dictionary of the Terms Ancient and Modern of the Canting Crew, in its Several Tribes, of Gypsies, Beggars, Thieves, Cheats, with an Addition of Some Proverbs, Phrases, Figurative Speeches* by Anonymous. I recommend this book if you're looking for a 16th century synonym for almost any word. I would also have been lost without my map of *Tudor London: The City and Southwark in 1520*, published by the London Topographical Society.

This fall, my husband and I had the pleasure of visiting St. Bartholomew's Church in Green's Norton. The rector of this ancient church took the time to show us around and give us a detailed history of this incredible place. I especially enjoyed seeing the brass plaques and effigies of the many Greenes associated with Green's Norton. Although Nick Greene was not a real person, his ancestors were, including Katherine Parr, who later became Henry VIII's sixth and last wife. I highly recommend a visit to this wonderful church in Northamptonshire.

Additionally, I would like to thank Sharpe Books for taking a chance on my debut novel, *A Knight's Duty,* and who continue to enthusiastically publish my work. Also, many thanks to my brilliant early readers Christina Howard and Karen Rulison, whose insights and enthusiasm are unparalleled. My wonderful

THE FAILED APPRENTICE

husband Stuart read the many incarnations of *The Failed Apprentice* and was an excellent sounding board and cheerleader. Our son Rudy provided unlimited encouragement and positivity, and just a few eye rolls.

I am blessed to have a great group of friends in New York whose constant support and interest warms my heart every day. The Bark Lickers' friendship is a balm to my soul; I love you all and our time spent together, laughing until we cry. Also, special thanks to my college friends – a wonderfully supportive and remarkable group of women - the best out there!

Those who read my previous novel, *A Knight's Duty*, reviewed it, provided feedback, passed it along, and asked me to speak at their book clubs deserve a special acknowledgment. Heartfelt thanks to Pamela Hill Reilly who was the first to "book me" for her book club. The enthusiasm my debut novel received was overwhelming, and I thank each and every one of you who took a chance on it.

I love to connect with my readers! Please feel free to drop me a note at wjsmallauthor@gmail.com or stop by my website at wjsmallauthor.com. And be on the lookout for the next adventures of Will Patten, coming soon!

Printed in Great Britain
by Amazon